Join the Little House Family
Five Generations of Pioneer Girls

Martha Morse, Laura's great-grandmother
born 1782
Martha was born to a wealthy landowning family in
Scotland. She loved her family, but she also wanted to
see the world, and one day she left her home to start a
new life in America.

Charlotte Tucker, Laura's grandmother
born 1809
Martha's daughter Charlotte was born a city girl, and
grew up near the bustling port of Boston. Charlotte had
a restless spirit and traveled farther and farther west,
before settling in Wisconsin.

Caroline Quiner, Laura's mother
born 1839
Charlotte's daughter Caroline spent her childhood in
Wisconsin, and her days were busy helping her mother
keep their little frontier farm running. Caroline grew
up to be Ma Ingalls, Laura's mother.

Laura Ingalls
born 1867
Caroline's daughter Laura traveled by covered wagon
across the frontier. When Laura grew up, she realized
the ways of the pioneer were ending and wrote down the
stories of her childhood in the Little House books.

Rose Wilder, Laura's daughter
born 1886
Laura's daughter, Rose, traveled from South Dakota to
the Ozark Mountains of Missouri. She grew up hearing
the stories of her mother's frontier girlhood and determined that one day she would be a new kind of pioneer.

Rose
and her mother, Laura

Martha
(1782–1862)

Betsy	Lewis	Linus	Lydia	Thomas	**Charlotte**
(b. 1800)	(b. 1802)	(b. 1803)	(b. 1805)	(b. 1807)	(1809–1884)

Martha	Joseph	Henry	Martha
(1832–1836)	(1834–1862)	(1835–1882)	(1837–1927)

Mary   **Laura**   *m.*   Almanzo Wilder
(1865–1928)   **(1867–1957)**   (1857–1949)

Rose
(1886–1968)

The Little House Family Tree

m.   Lewis Tucker

m.   Henry Quiner (1807–1844)   Caroline (b. 1811)   Mary (b. 1813)   Nancy (b. 1816)   George (1820–1821)

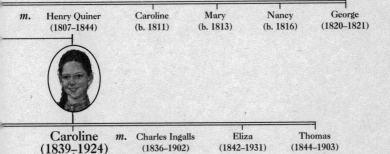

Caroline (1839–1924)   *m.*   Charles Ingalls (1836–1902)   Eliza (1842–1931)   Thomas (1844–1903)

Caroline (1870–1946)   Charles (1875–1876)   Grace (1877–1941)

Little Town *in* the Ozarks

Roger Lea MacBride

Illustrated by David Gilleece

HarperTrophy®

A Division of HarperCollinsPublishers

To Vivian Glover and Connie Tidwell,
who joyfully kept house for so many
Little House and Rocky Ridge readers

Harper Trophy®, ®, Little House®, and The Rose Years™
are trademarks of HarperCollins Publishers Inc.

Little Town in the Ozarks
Text copyright © 1996 by the Estate of Roger Lea MacBride
Illustrations copyright © 1996 by David Gilleece
Library of Congress Cataloging-in-Publication Data
MacBride, Roger Lea, 1929–1995
    Little town in the Ozarks / Roger Lea MacBride ; illustrated by David
Gilleece.
        p.   cm.
    Summary: When drought and fire afflict Rocky Ridge Farm, eleven-
year-old Rose Wilder and her parents temporarily move to Mansfield and
try to adjust to a new life in town.
    ISBN 0-06-024977-3. — ISBN 0-06-024970-6 (lib. bdg.)
    ISBN 0-06-440580-X (pbk.)
    1. Wilder, Laura Ingalls, 1867–1957—Juvenile fiction.   [1. Wilder, Laura
Ingalls, 1867–1957—Fiction.   2. Frontier and pioneer life—Missouri—
Fiction.   3. Farm life—Missouri—Fiction.   4. Missouri—Fiction.]
I. Gilleece, David, ill.   II. Title.
PZ7.M12255Lit   1996   95-47590
[Fic]—dc20   CIP
                                                                                      AC
Typography by Alicia Mikles

❖

Dear Reader:

The book you hold in your hands is the work of my father, Roger Lea MacBride. It continues the childhood story of Rose Wilder Lane, and her mother and father, Laura Ingalls and Almanzo Wilder. Rose treated my father much as she would have treated a grandson and told him many stories about what it was like growing up in Missouri almost a hundred years ago. Dad took those stories and spun them into a series of books based on the facts of Rose's life. Little Town in the Ozarks *is the fifth of those books.*

I'm sorry to have to tell you that my father has passed away. But my sadness is softened some because his work, the stories of Rose's early life, will continue. He left four partially completed manuscripts that continue Rose's tale, right up to the time she is seventeen years old and ready to leave home to start a life of her own.

There will be three more books after this. With the help of the editors at HarperCollins, we will be able to complete the story of Rose and her family as they come into the modern age of the telephone and automobile.

I am very pleased that these stories will be available to new generations of readers. You will find, as I did, that in a hundred years the things young people think and worry about haven't changed all that much.

Abigail MacBride Allen

Contents

Little Town
in the Ozarks

A Noisy, Crowded Place

The whistle of the Stockman's Special shrieked its warning as it raced westward toward town. On the back stoop, Fido flattened his ears, threw his head back, and began to howl. The windows of the little house in town had been opened to air, and through every one Rose heard other town dogs answering the locomotive's mournful wail in their most wolfish voices.

"Aaooooooooow! Aaooooooooow!"

The sound of all that baying made the skin on Rose's arms prickle with gooseflesh. She wondered what the dogs were crying about,

1

what the train's whistle said that stirred them up so.

An instant later Bunting let out a ferocious bellow from the stock pen.

Rose looked out the kitchen window she was cleaning. The passing locomotive made the glass quiver and the frame tremble with a small rattling sound. The railroad tracks ran nearly right through the backyard of the Wilders' new home in town.

"There goes that durn cow again!" Papa cried out. With a loud *clunk!* he set down the heavy trunk he was carrying in from the dining room and dashed out the back door. Rose threw down her rag and ran after him to see if she could help.

"Mind she doesn't kick you!" Mama called out from the bedroom, where Mrs. Cooley was helping her tuck fresh sheets on the bed.

Out the back door of the kitchen, in the little stock lot at the foot of the railroad grade, poor Bunting thrashed her head from side to side. She tugged the rope and tried to jerk her picket pin out of the ground. Her wet nose puffed little clouds of steam in the chill autumn air. Her hind feet kicked up clods of dull red mud. She stretched her neck and bellowed pitifully again, her dark eyes bulging with terror.

Papa opened the gate and grabbed her rope. He held it tight, digging in his heels and trying to talk sense into her.

"Easy girl, easy," he crooned. "Nothing to be afraid of. Whoa, now."

The air trembled again with the cry of the express train's whistle. The ground quaked a little under Rose's feet as the great iron monster roared out from behind a row of trees. Its pillar of gray-white smoke billowed from the stack like an angry storm cloud. It rode high up on the grade, higher than the house, its metal wheels screeching against the rails. A string of freight cars rumbled behind.

Two boys ran laughing up to the alley fence to watch. Rose knew one of them, Scott Coday. He was a brother of Rose's friend Blanche. Blanche was Rose's seatmate in school. She was already twelve years old. Rose would have her eleventh birthday in December.

Scott pushed a shiny new bicycle, the first one Rose had ever seen, except in pictures in the Sears, Roebuck catalogue. A bicycle could cost twenty-five dollars. Just to see one was really something. She couldn't imagine how you could ride it without falling.

"Lookit that dumb old cow!" Scott crowed, stepping on the fence's crossbar to see better. "She don't know a plain lockee-motive from a pack o' wild varmints."

Rose glared at those boys with their smirking grins. She wanted to tell Scott to go stand on someone else's fence, and to scold him for gawking at other folks' business. But before she could speak, Papa cried out, "Run and fetch a bit of corn, Rose! Might calm her some."

Rose dashed into the dusty little barn—it wasn't much bigger than a shed, really—and grabbed a handful of kernels from an open feed sack. Poor Bunting hated living in town. The little stock lot was so small, and the barn so cramped, that Papa had had to leave her calf, Spark, out on Rocky Ridge Farm. Bunting was used to having Spark's company, and having pastures to roam and explore, and horses and chickens and Fido and the cat, Blackfoot, to chase and pretend to be frightened by.

Town was crowded and noisy, and the poor cow was terrified of the trains. Papa didn't dare put her in her stall; she might kick the walls out trying to run away. So he had kept her picketed in the stock pen until she could hear the noisy locomotives without bolting.

Rose didn't know if she liked to live in town either. When they had driven the wagon to their new home that very morning, to bring the last of their things from the farm, the neighbors had swarmed out of their houses to watch. Then the women brought platters of fried chicken and pies and corn bread. Some of the men had helped Papa and the Wilders' hired man, Abe Baird, move the heavy things into the house.

Everyone had been very friendly, and curious. The women brought their dishes to the porch and talked with Mama, peering over her shoulder at the trunks and clothing, and the furniture that looked rather shabby out of its proper place, all piled in the yard and on the porch.

"You'll find this a good, clean-living town, Mrs. Wilder," a woman with quick, squirrelly eyes told Mama. "The children can get to be peevish now and then. You know how mischief loves the young'uns. But the neighbors are right proper folks."

"I have admired this house since the time Mr. Masters built it," a man told Papa. "I was sorry to hear of the bad turn of luck you had on your farm. Seems there's hardly any future left in farming."

"This your little girl?" an old woman with hollow cheeks and shriveled lips asked Mama. "I guess she's smart as a whip, ain't she? My granddaughter says she's so smart, she don't come to school half the time."

Rose blushed, but not with pleasure. She didn't like to be talked about as if she weren't even there.

Mama and Papa were very polite to everyone.

"We're still farmers, even if we live in town," Papa said, chuckling. "Our hired man is living in the house with his family, and we'll be out there ourselves any chance we get, keeping the place up."

"Rose is a bright girl," Mama said in her best company voice. "And she keeps her lessons up at home, even when she must miss school to help with the farm chores."

As they walked back to their own houses, the women huddled in twos, their heads bent together.

Rose hated to have all those people staring at them, measuring them with their questions and restless eyes. She wasn't friends with any of the children who stayed on the sidewalk looking at her through the hitching rail and giggling at each other's jokes.

Rose felt sorry for Bunting, cooped up in her tiny stock pen. Even though she herself had yet to spend a single night away from the farm—not once in three years—she already missed living in the country, where the only prying eyes belonged to the animals and there was room to breathe.

She crept up to Bunting and held out the kernels in her open hand. The Jersey cow looked at Rose with wide eyes and sniffed. She stretched her neck and let out one last complaining moan. Then she nuzzled a wet mouthful from Rose's palm and stood crunching, her tail switching nervously as the fading whistle floated back from the far side of town, where the train raced the lowering sun.

Papa stroked Bunting's soft brown neck and scratched behind one of her restless ears. "That's my girl. You'll get used to it in time."

All in a single day, Rose's life had changed. She and Mama and Papa were moving into the house in Mansfield that Grandfather Wilder had bought for them that summer. For three years Rose had lived on Rocky Ridge Farm, a mile outside of town, helping Mama and Papa build up the place and tending the young apple orchard.

That summer, a killing drought had stunted the crops. A fire started by sparks from the hot brakes of a passing train had reached all the way to their farm and burned over some of the fields. The neighbors had come and helped save the precious orchard. In a few more years, if all went well, the apple trees would bear their first harvest, and then Mama and Papa could have most anything they could want.

For now they couldn't scratch a living from the thin, stony soil. They decided that until the trees were old enough to bear, they would live in the house in town.

After Papa's friend Mr. Cooley was killed in a train wreck, Papa bought his draywagon from Mrs. Cooley. Papa was going to be the new drayman now, hauling freight to and from the railroad depot.

Mama would work, too, keeping books for Mr. Waters' oil company; and they might take in boarders in the extra rooms. With Mama's egg money, and what crops and timber they could harvest from the farm in their spare time, they could have enough money to pay the mortgage on Rocky Ridge and to hold on until the first apples could be picked and shipped.

The new house was very big, with six rooms, not counting Rose's attic bedroom. Six doors opened to the outside, and there were more windows than Rose could count.

The little house on Rocky Ridge Farm was just two downstairs rooms and Rose's attic room. It was cozy as a bird's nest. The new house was empty and felt cold as a cave. Rose's heavy shoes made hollow clomping sounds when she walked through the barren rooms.

"I don't know as we'll ever have furniture enough to fill them all," Mama fretted. "I finally have room for a parlor and not a thing for it."

Rose had lived in a town before, on the prairie in South Dakota. But she was a little girl then, and that town, De Smet, was small, quiet, and uncrowded. It had a railroad depot, but only two or three trains passed through each day, and the tracks were far from where she lived.

A dozen or more trains roared by the back of their house in Mansfield every day, spreading plumes of bitter coal smoke and greasy clinker dust.

"In a week or so, you won't even notice them," Mrs. Cooley said in a faraway voice.

Rose was helping Mama wipe the dishes before putting them away in their places in the cabinets. "Except for the soot, of course," Mrs. Cooley added, as if suddenly remembering that she was not alone. "Often times I have to dust the sills every other day."

Mrs. Cooley sank back into her thoughts. She gazed out the kitchen window and sighed. Rose stole a glance at Mama. Her mouth pinched as she stood in thought for a moment, and her chest heaved with a silent sigh.

It was only a few months since Mr. Cooley died. The memory of that black day was still fresh in all their minds, all the more so because this was the house where Mr. and Mrs. Cooley had lived with their sons, Paul and George, who were Rose's friends. Grandfather Wilder bought the house from Mrs. Cooley after Mr. Cooley had died; then he deeded it over to Mama and Papa.

The Cooleys were the Wilders' best friends. They had driven in wagons three years ago with Rose, Mama, and Papa, all the way from South Dakota to Mansfield, Missouri, in the

Ozark Mountains. Now Mrs. Cooley was a widow with a family to raise. It was a frightening thing to be a woman alone with children to feed.

Rose looked around the kitchen and wondered if she would ever forget that Mr. Cooley had taken his meals there, and scolded Paul and George for their mischief, and teased Mrs. Cooley about her cooking. The memory of him lurked in every corner.

"I don't mind housework," said Mama, sinking into a kitchen chair to rest a moment. She kicked off her shoes and rubbed the bottoms of her feet. "But this is a big house to keep. I just hope it doesn't get the best of me."

Just then there was a knocking at the front door.

"Oh my! More visitors!" Mama groaned, slipping her shoes back on and tucking a stray wisp of brown hair behind her ear. "We've had more callers today than in three years of living on the farm. At this rate we'll never get the kitchen put right."

What Would People Think?

Nearly everyone they knew in town stopped by to pay their respects that day, and even some they didn't know. The new minister from Prairie Hollow Church, Reverend Davis, came with Mrs. Davis, who brought a box of cinnamon cookies she had baked.

"I hope we'll be seeing you folks in church more, now that you'll be living in town," Reverend Davis said. He was very tall and dressed in a fine black suit with a crisply starched collar. He tilted his head a little to

13

the side as he spoke, the way a grown-up does when speaking to a child.

Looking up at him, Rose could see tufts of long hairs in his nostrils mixing with his mustache. It made her feel odd inside, and she had to look away.

"And it would be a good thing, too, for Rose," Mrs. Davis chirped, clasping her white-gloved hands together and giving Rose a thin, empty smile. "Proper Sunday schooling will help bring the Lord into her young life."

Rose stole a glance at Mama. Mama had never made her go to Sunday school, and the way Mrs. Davis said it made Rose hate the idea, the same as she disliked teachers who told her what to think. In that way Rose was just like Mama; she liked to make up her own mind about things.

Mama stiffened and drew up her short body ever so slightly. Her blue eyes flashed for an instant. Then she wiped hands, red from lye soap, on her old patched apron. "Yes," she said crisply. "It will be useful to be so near to everything, although we still have our farm and orchard that need tending. We are farmers first and last. As for Rose, I have found parents to be God's most gifted ministers."

"Of course," Reverend Davis said earnestly, shifting his feet and fingering the brim of his hat. "We only meant that . . . Well, Mrs. Wilder. We just wanted you to know, the doors of our church are open to your family whenever you may wish to come."

"I thank you kindly for the cookies," Mama said. "I'm sure we will enjoy them."

Mama showed Reverend and Mrs. Davis to the gate, then marched back up the walk, onto the little porch, brushing by Rose.

"Come along," she said as she swung the door open. "We've got work to do if ever we're to get supper on the table. And Bunting yet to be milked."

Rose looked around the kitchen as they finished the last of the cold chicken one of the neighbors had brought. On the counters and extra chairs and the clothing trunk sat pies and plates of cookies and a jar of pickles and a crock of sausage.

15

She munched one of Mrs. Davis' cinnamon cookies. It was dry and sandy, and had the bitter aftertaste of molasses sweetening. Rose stuck it in the pocket of her apron, to give to Fido later.

Papa got up to dish himself another helping of Mrs. Rippee's persimmon pudding, and to close the windows.

"Feels like we might get our first hard frost tonight," he said. "I reckon Stubbins'll be butchering before long." Mr. Stubbins owned the farm nearest Rocky Ridge.

Alva Stubbins was Rose's first friend in Missouri. They had been the best of friends. But one day Rose had accidentally embarrassed Alva, and everything had changed. Alva had no interest in book learning, and she didn't like the town girls one bit. As the two had grown older, and Rose had made friends in school, they had drifted apart. They almost never played together anymore.

From the depot nearby came the ringing bell and chuffing cough of a local train as it pulled out, then its grunting and huffing as it passed behind the house heading east. Bunting lowed once. The local trains didn't scare her as much as the roaring expresses.

Mama looked around the kitchen and sighed tiredly. "I hardly know what to think. Everyone has been so neighborly, and yet I can't help it; I don't like to be beholden to folks.

"And how can a body get any work done with all this commotion? Now we have all these extra dishes to wash and return, and kindnesses to be repaid."

"You're just a bit wrought up from the move," Papa said.

"It's true," answered Mama, going to the stove to pour hot water into the teapot. "I was so at my wits' end today that I fear I was rude to Reverend and Mrs. Davis. I miss the peacefulness of the farm, Manly. You know I don't like to live in towns, among folks we hardly know. The sooner we can move back to the farm, the better I'll like it."

"Me too," Rose interrupted. "I don't like it here."

"It's a change, girls," said Papa. "We all have

to get used to living with close neighbors. Town is another world from being out on the farm. It'll take some time, is all. You'll see.

"Now I've got to run down to the depot and see if there's any freight that needs hauling from Number One-oh-five."

Rose slept her first night in the house on her straw tick on the floor of her new attic room. Papa had been so busy, he hadn't found time to put together her bedstead, but Rose didn't care. Her body was so tired and achy from a long day of carrying things and scrubbing floors and washing windows that she could have fallen asleep right on the hard floor.

Her room was above Mama and Papa's room. It had slanty unpainted ceilings and beams that were the undersides of the roof, and two windows looking out the back of the house on the stock lot and the railroad grade. To get in and out of her room, she had to climb a straight-up ladder that was nailed to the wall of Mama and Papa's room.

As tired as she was, Rose's thoughts fluttered

about like nervous chickens just before a storm. She listened to the little creakings of the new house, and the sounds of the neighborhood. Somewhere nearby a door shut. A moment later, a gate latched and footsteps crunched on the gravel sidewalk. Fido barked twice. A baby cried out. Horses' hooves galloped past on Commercial Street.

Through the floorboards Rose could hear the murmur of Mama's lively voice talking softly to Papa the way she did every night before they went to bed.

" . . . Don't like having to keep up appearances . . . work to do . . . miss the sunsets . . ."

Papa's answers came in short, deep rumbles that Rose couldn't make out.

A mouse scrabbled along a rafter somewhere toward the front of the house. That made Rose miss Blackfoot, her orange cat. She had wanted to bring her to town, but Papa said they needed to have a cat on the farm.

"Who will keep the mice and rats out of the corncrib?" he asked. "Besides, cats don't much like to live in a new place. She'll be happier staying on Rocky Ridge, and you'll see her every time you're there."

The faces of the people who had visited that day flipped through her mind's eye like a stack of pictures. She kept coming back to the minister and his wife. Rose had rarely seen Mama as irritable with strangers as she was with Reverend and Mrs. Davis. Rose was very glad she didn't have to go to Sunday school.

In South Dakota everybody—Mama, Papa, Rose, Grandma and Grandpa Ingalls, and all of Rose's aunts—went to the Congregational church that Grandpa had helped build before Rose was born, when the little town on the prairie was brand-new.

In Mansfield there was only one church. All of the best families in town belonged—families like Blanche's who owned the stores and the bank and rode to church in brass-trimmed buggies and wore the finest clothing money could buy. Mama said the church in town was not so very different from a Congregational church.

But Rose heard her tell Papa one Sunday night, "I've never seen such finery as those folks wear to church. Makes me shy to be seen in my same best dress two Sundays in a row, as if it's just about a sin to be poor. I wish someone would raise a church for simple people like us."

Farm families like Rose's usually went to other small churches, in log houses tucked away in the forests. But Mama said those ministers gave noisy sermons, and she didn't like to hear preaching that was full of fire and brimstone. "I can hear God's word plain enough without its being shouted at me," she said. "It's there every day in the sunrise and the songs of the birds."

But she did sometimes like to put on her best dress, hear a good sermon, sing, and visit with the folks in town. And Papa liked to show off his beautifully groomed Morgan mares, May and Pet, and swap gossip with the other men.

So some Sundays they went to church. Afterward Mama visited with Mrs. Cooley and some of the other town women, and Papa stood outside with the men talking crop prices and weather.

Rose liked to sing also, and to see her friend

Blanche, and Paul and George Cooley. But she didn't care much for preaching, especially on hot summer days when her skin prickled and sweat ran down the nape of her neck.

Most Sundays they stayed home. "A church is God between four walls," said Mama. Besides, there always were farm chores that never had a day of rest, or a sick animal to care for. Sometimes the road into town was so covered with ice or thick with mud that it was impossible to travel.

Even if they didn't go to church, Mama always read the Bible aloud to Rose and Papa after breakfast, the beautiful round tones of her voice rising and falling like the sweetest hymn.

Rose's heart sank when she thought about those quiet, peaceful Sundays on Rocky Ridge Farm. She thought about the little house that Papa had built. Now Abe Baird, the hired man, lived in it with his wife, Effie, their twin babies, and Abe's little brother, Swiney.

She missed Swiney and the fun they always had together. She especially missed going barefoot.

"You know I like to go without shoes as much as you," Mama had said as they laid out the rag rug on the kitchen floor. "That was all right on the farm, where all we saw were each other. But what would folks think, a grown woman traipsing around in her dirty bare feet? It just isn't done."

"But I'm not a grown woman."

"You're a grown-up girl," said Mama. "Push that corner a little over to the left. There. You're grown up enough to mind your mother without making a pouty face. Now let's move the table."

As she lay in bed, Rose felt the walls of the whole world closing in around her, stealing the very breath of life from her lungs. She missed the ghostly nights with the wind sighing in the trees outside her bedroom, a lonely owl hooting somewhere off in the forest, and the horses nickering softly in their stalls.

Rose wondered how she could ever get accustomed to living in town.

Hoover's Junk Pile

"That's Miss Sarah," Blanche whispered. "She boards up at the Helfinstines', by the schoolhouse. You know, she's an *old maid*!" she hissed.

Blanche's breath tickled Rose's ear unbearably, and she felt her face grow hot. Rose was shocked at the things Blanche said about people, and practically right out loud.

Miss Sarah was passing in front of Rose's house, picking her way along the rough gravel sidewalk toward town, holding her hem up from the frosty mud in one hand and her market basket in the other. It had rained during the night, and then frozen. Her shoes crackled the thin layer of ice.

Rose had to look away.

When she had passed by, Blanche sang a mean ditty:

> "*Red and yellow, red and yellow,*
>   *Ugly old maid,*
>   *Can't catch a fellow.*"

But Miss Sarah did not look ugly, or old. She was only a dressed-up lady walking along the street on her way to trade in town.

Mama's sister Mary was an old maid. "What's so awful about being an old maid?" Rose wanted to know.

Blanche stood up from where they were sitting on the edge of the porch and hopscotched a few steps down the walk. "I don't know," she said with a shrug and a flounce of her curly black hair. "But Mother says they're poor things who can't help it, and people ought to be sorry for them. Miss Sarah's twenty-four years old. She'll never have a husband now."

Blanche had stopped by for a visit after breakfast chores. Rose should have invited her in; that was the polite thing to do. But she was ashamed of the barren, untidy house.

Blanche lived in one of the most beautiful houses in town. It had two whole floors filled with lovely scalloped davenports with lace antimacassars and gleaming polished tables with doilies and painted globe lamps and seashells, and carpets on all the floors.

There was nothing to see in Rose's new house except a few rag carpets, the simple table and chairs and whatnot that Papa had made with his own hands, Mama's rocking chair, and the kitchen still cluttered with pots and pans piled in the corner.

So Rose and Blanche sat outside in the warming sunlight. It was Saturday, and they chattered away as a parade of wagons rattled past, heading toward the town square, each one driven by a farmer in his best home-sewn jacket over patched overalls and a dusty hat. A woman sat on the seat beside him, her crisp calico bonnet covering her face like a morning glory blossom.

"I would hate to have to wear a bonnet," Blanche said. "It would just squash my curls. You really ought to curl your hair, Rose. Simply everyone wears it that way now."

Rose fingered the end of her long braid. She'd started wearing her light-brown hair as Mama did at home, instead of in two braids the way Rose used to. She liked her braid, but she felt her face grow warm at Blanche's words.

Over the edges of the wagon boxes, children draped themselves like wriggling puppies in a crate. From under the boys' shaggy haircuts and tattered hats, and the girls' floppy bonnets, their eager eyes looked out at everything. Rose knew that the girls' starched pinafores hid the patches on their dresses.

The wagons creaked under their loads of cooped hens and butter jars, barrels of apples and sacks of potatoes—all the things each family had grown or raised or trapped, being brought to town to trade for their salt, dress goods, shoes, and farm tools.

Rose looked at those wagons and realized with a shock that she was seeing herself, and

Mama and Papa. She remembered all the times they had gotten up in the dark, fed and watered their livestock, eaten a quick, cold breakfast, scrubbed their faces and hands, and driven over the bumpy, hilly roads to come to town.

Her heart ached with knowing just how those children felt, how much they looked forward to a trip to town, where they could see the crowds of wagons and horses and people milling about the square.

The boys might play mumblety-peg with their knives in the town square and then get into a scrap with some town boys who would call them country jakes and make fun of their clothes. The girls would stare longingly through the store windows at spools of brightly colored ribbon and dolls with real hair, and gape with awe at the women bustling about on errands wearing feathered hats and carrying dainty parasols.

They would hope for a train to come sliding into the depot, its bell clanging. Then they would scream with pleasure when the locomotive belched a cloud of steam with a deafening roar. There would be a trip to Reynolds' or Nelson's, where the store clerks would give them each a peppermint stick or a little bag of lemon drops.

Rose ached with remembering the time she went to town with Mama and Papa and some town girls made fun of her for being a country girl. That memory still smarted.

"I'm so glad you live in town now, Rose," Blanche bubbled happily. She pulled a bit of thread from the lace cuff of her blue wool dress. Without thinking, Rose tucked her apron around her knees, to hide the stain of spilled bacon grease that no amount of scrubbing could get out.

"Now we can visit any old time we want. And there's so much to do and see. I know!" she shouted. "Let's walk down to the square! We can go to Father's drugstore and get some candy."

"I have to ask Mama," said Rose. A tingle of dread crept up her legs. She wanted to go more than anything, but she couldn't walk with Blanche in her old chore dress. Besides, she could already hear Mama's disapproving voice.

"To the square? I should think not," said Mama, wringing the mop out into the bucket. She was finishing up the floor in the pantry, just off the dining room. "There's the sweeping and dusting to be done, and the cow to be led to pasture. Besides, I won't have you gadding about like a ragamuffin, getting yourself nearly run down. The way some of these men drive, it's a wonder more people aren't hurt. The square is no place for a girl to be playing."

The mop slid back and forth across the smooth dining room floor. They had washed it with lye soap, and now it shone bright as gold.

"There are children living all around us now. Why don't you make friends and play with them in the alley?"

"I don't want to be friends with them," Rose grumbled. "Anyway, I already have Blanche to be a friend."

"There will be time enough for visiting." Mama huffed as she wrung out the mop again.

"School starts soon. Then you'll see Blanche every day. You run and tell her you've got chores to do, then fetch a clean rag. I want to get this floor dry so we can move the table and chairs in."

When Rose got back out to the porch, Blanche was leaning over the gate talking with Lois Beaumont, a girl Rose knew from school but never had played with. Lois was thirteen years old and very grown-up.

"Come along, Rose. We'll all go together," Blanche called out. Rose walked slowly down the path. Lois was smartly dressed in a crisp green-and-white-plaid skirt with a brilliantly white shirtwaist with a wide starched collar. Over the waist she wore a beautiful green silk jacket with gold braiding down the front and on the cuffs.

"Mama says I must stay and help with the chores," Rose mumbled.

"Oh well, then." Blanche shrugged. "I suppose we'll be going."

"Hello," said Lois, holding out her hand to be shaken. She smiled sweetly and Rose shook it, feeling the warm, soft palm. Rose clenched her rough hands and jammed them into the pockets of her apron.

"Hello," Rose answered.

"Lois' father is Mr. Beaumont. He owns the bank," Blanche said proudly. "Beaumont is a French name. It means 'beautiful mountain.'"

"Oh you be quiet, Blanche," Lois scolded. "Come on, let's go. It's tiresome just standing here."

Blanche and Lois sauntered off down the street, arm in arm, giggling together about something. Rose watched them go, and her chest heaved with a sigh of yearning.

After she had finished wiping the water from the dining-room floor, Mama sent her to lead Bunting out to pasture. Papa had shown her where the gate was, on the road that led to Rocky Ridge Farm. Another farmer owned that field, but he let some of the townspeople use it for grazing.

The cow eagerly followed Rose out of the stock lot at a trot, the bell around her neck ringing with each step. When they got out on the street, though, she tugged on her lead every few steps to stop and nibble at the weeds growing in the ditches.

"Darn cow!" Rose muttered. She got a stick and gave Bunting a sharp poke on her flank to get her going. Bunting looked at Rose balefully, switched her tail, and went right back to nibbling. The cow was too big, and Rose too small, for Rose to pull her along. Bunting was stubborn, and it took Rose a long time to get her to the edge of town, where the telephone poles ended, the road left the last house behind, and open fields began.

The street was aflame with the colors of freshly fallen leaves. The trees were shedding their beautiful coats, and soon all that would be left would be a carpet of brown rotting leaves and bare branches.

Rose was in a snappish mood. As soon as she got out of sight of the house, she stopped to take off her shoes and stockings. She knotted the laces together, tucked the stockings inside the shoes, and hung them over her shoulder.

Her feet rejoiced to feel the cool, damp earth again, and kick up little clouds of leaves. It was refreshing to be out in the crisp autumn air and hear the last of the crickets chirping their slow, mournful songs in the dry grass, and watch the cloud shadows chase each other across the rolling hills.

Her unhappy thoughts piled up like storm clouds. Watching Blanche walk off with Lois, Rose had never felt so left behind, so alone.

She thought about how, living on the farm, she was the center of her whole world. In fact, every living thing on the farm knew that the universe had been created just for itself.

The horses knew that their stables, the fields, and the creek were there just to keep them fed, watered, and cozy. Papa was there to currycomb them when they were tired and lathery, and bring them blankets on the bitter cold winter nights.

Even a turtle crawling clumsily over fallen trees and rocks looked at the world through fierce eyes that knew the trees and sky and earth had been put there just for its pleasure.

Now the center of Rose's world had moved off somewhere else, and she couldn't find it. She didn't even know where to look.

She and Bunting finally reached the pasture gate. She opened it, and as soon as she had untied Bunting's lead, the cow ambled off into the field sniffing for something green to eat.

When she had shut the gate again, Rose looked off across the little valley of Fry Creek, toward Rocky Ridge Farm. She could hear Abe's axe ringing in the woodlot. She wanted more than anything to visit with the Bairds, to see the house and play with Effie's twin babies, but Mama expected her to come straight home.

She was just about to turn and walk back over the low hill toward town when she heard a voice shouting, "Rose! Hey Rose!"

Down the slope toward Fry Creek, coming out of a thicket, Swiney was running through the weeds. It took him a long time to reach her, thrashing through the undergrowth, and he was all out of breath.

"Hey Rose," he gasped. "Whatcha doin'?"

"I took the cow to pasture. What're you doing?"

"Catchin' crawdads in the creek. Want to come with me?" Swiney was a sight, with his ragged pants wet at the hem, patched jacket, and unruly hair sticking out from under his straw hat. But his eyes shone with excitement, and Rose was very glad to see his beaming, freckled face.

"I don't know," Rose began slowly, glancing over her shoulder. "Mama expects me home."

"Aw, c'mon," Swiney said. He took a dried milkweed pod from its stem, broke it open, and blew away the fluff. A stiff breeze sent the seeds dancing across the field. "Just for a spell."

"I can't," Rose insisted. "We haven't finished cleaning the new house."

"Well, least you can come along and see the trash pile I found. It's crammed with handy junk. It's just over yonder, by that walnut tree."

Rose wavered for a moment. She didn't care much about an old junk pile, but she thought a little fun might cheer her up.

She could tell Mama that Bunting got away and it took extra time to catch her again. That was a lie. Rose never lied, not once since the awful time she got Abe in trouble with Effie by telling a bald-faced fib.

But just this once, a very small lie, hardly a lie at all, wouldn't matter. It *had* taken her a long time to drag the cow to pasture.

"All right," she finally said. Rose dropped her shoes on the ground and flew halfway down the hill behind Swiney. Just under the gnarly walnut tree rose a pile of old barrels, crates, rusted horseshoes, and old wagon wheels. Swiney lifted an old bleached-gray wagon wheel and pushed it down the hill. It rolled crazily, wobbling, faster and faster until it smashed into a tree trunk and the spokes shattered into splinters.

"YAHOO!" Swiney screamed. Then he picked up a horseshoe and flung it as far as he could.

"This is the place Mr. Hoover throws out his trash from the livery stable," Swiney said excitedly. "You could make most anything from it. A fort, or even a little wagon. Look here," he said, tugging a barrel upright. "It ain't even broke. Roll me around, Rose."

Swiney clambered inside and Rose pushed him a little ways down the hill. She had to struggle to push it over the bumps.

"Faster, faster," Swiney demanded, his voice sounding as if it were in a cave.

"I can't," said Rose. "It's too heavy."

Swiney crawled out. "You get inside. I'll show you. It's fun."

Rose got inside the barrel and sat down. It was dank and musty, but cozy to sit in and look at the circle of light outside.

Swiney's broad upside-down face peered in at her. "Push up with your hands, up here, and down with your feet," he said. "That way you'll go round with the barrel."

Rose braced herself, and Swiney began to roll the barrel. Slowly she turned upside down, pushing with all her might to keep from tumbling. The circle of bright outdoors turned upside down with her. Then her dress fell over her face, and she couldn't see anything.

Her stomach flip-flopped, but she didn't feel sick, just giddy. She began to giggle. Then her dress fell away and she was right-side up again, going back upside down, faster this time. She tried looking out the open end of the barrel, but it was a blur of weeds and sunshine, spinning around, faster and faster.

She felt her hands slipping, and her feet, too. Her stomach sank, and a queasiness leaped into her throat. The barrel bumped hard against something, and the back of Rose's head banged painfully against the staves.

"Swiney, stop!" Rose shouted. "You're scaring me! It's going too fast."

But the barrel only rolled faster. Dimly she heard Swiney's voice shouting. She couldn't keep her hands and feet in place. She began to tumble against the hard wooden sides. The barrel flung her about like a rag doll. She banged her head again, and then her elbow.

The circle of light whirled. She couldn't tell if she was up or down or sideways; she was just tumbling and banging. She was too mixed up and terrified even to scream.

Crash! The barrel hit something. Wood cracked and shattered. Everything stopped.

She heard water gurgling. One side of her felt cool and wet. She couldn't move. Her ears buzzed like bees in a jar. Her head ached. She was afraid to open her eyes. Rose thought she might be dead.

The Eyes of Strangers

Rose felt her forehead; it was sticky wet. She looked at her hand; it was covered with blood. Pieces of broken barrel slats lay all around her. Then she heard splashing, and Swiney's worried face looked down at her.

Poor Swiney burst into tears. He, too, had thought she might be dead.

When Rose could finally speak and sit up, he helped her wash off. The cut on her head wasn't so bad after all. Her knee hurt, but it was just skinned.

"I'll be all right," she said in a quavery voice. "I just want to go home now."

"Aw, Rose. I'm real sorry," Swiney sobbed. He dabbed Rose's forehead with the cuff of his jacket. Rose saw the fresh blood on the cloth, but she didn't shed a single tear.

"I'm real sorry. The darn barrel got away from me, is all. It just rolled away, right down the hill into the creek. I tried to catch it, but it was rolling too fast. You got to believe me. I didn't mean to smash you up."

"Please don't cry. I know you didn't mean to," said Rose. The cold creek water and the wet dress against her skin helped wake her up. But she still felt woolly-headed. "It was fun before that. I'd best be going. Mama'll be worrying."

Rose limped back to the road, put on her stockings and shoes, and hurried down the hill into town. Her head ached, and a sharp pain stabbed her knee each time she stepped on her right foot. But no pain could be worse than the one Rose felt knowing how upset Mama would be.

When she passed the Murrays' house, Mrs. Murray jumped up from her rocking chair on the porch. "Oh my!" she cried, rushing down the path to the gate. "Child, are you all right?"

"Yes'm," Rose said, and hurried on. But a sob jerked from her throat. She heard other voices exclaiming from other porches and yards: "Lookit her!"

A little boy who was playing with a ball in the street stopped to stare, but she was too ashamed to look up until she got to her own house. Then she dashed down the alley, through the back gate, and ducked in the back door.

There was no lying to be done. When Rose limped into the house, Mama cried out in horror, and Rose finally could weep. It took her a long time to explain herself, while Mama cleaned her wounds and dabbed coal oil on them. Her mouth made a thin, tight line, and her blue eyes were as cold as her voice. Rose could hardly look at her.

"I declare, how could you do something so foolish? Didn't I tell you to come home straightaway? Aren't there enough dangers in the world without making up new ones?"

Finally Mama sat back in her chair. Her shoulders sagged, and she sighed wearily. Rose dared to look at her, and a fresh flood of tears spilled from her eyes. "I'm sorry, Mama," she said, snuffling. "Swiney didn't mean it; really he didn't. I just wanted to have a little bit of fun. I didn't know it would be dangerous."

"No, I suppose you didn't," Mama said gently. "But if you'd been doing as you were told, this never would have happened." She got up to put the teakettle on the stove. "You gave me the fright of my life, walking in here covered in blood. We could both do with something warm to drink."

Mama got Rose's second-best dress and made her change out of her wet, stained things. Then they sat together at the table, sipping from their cups. The warm, sweet tea soothed Rose, and when Mama started to tell a story, she knew everything was going to be all right.

It was about the time Mama nearly drowned in Plum Creek, when she was a little girl living in a dugout house in Minnesota. The way she told it sent shivers up Rose's spine. She could almost feel her arms ache when Mama told how hard it was to pull herself up onto a log from the raging water.

"One slip and I would have drowned for sure. It's a wonder any of us manage to make it through life," said Mama, "what with illness and disaster waiting around every bend.

"Well then, we'd best get back to work. Papa's bringing the chickens from the farm after supper, and I want to fix up some nests before he does."

They worked together in the tiny barn, putting old crates on some shelves and lining the crates with straw. All the time she worked, Rose was thinking. She loved the chores of farming, caring for the animals, making them cozy, bringing them their food and water.

They would have chickens in town, and Bunting. But she missed having the horses and mules nearby, and even her ill-tempered donkey, Spookendyke, and Abe and Effie to see 'most anytime, and the twins to tickle their tiny feet and make them laugh.

She thought a long time about everything,

and finally she got up the courage to speak her mind. "Mama, do you think I could stay out on the farm with Abe and Effie?"

Mama stopped in the middle of shaking a handful of straw into one of the crates and looked hard at Rose. "Instead of living here with Papa and me?"

"I was only thinking," Rose muttered. The look on Mama's face made her sorry she'd spoken.

"What were you thinking?" Mama grabbed another handful of straw and began to spread it on the floor.

Rose took a deep breath and let out all her complaints in a great flood of words and fresh tears. She hated living in town. Blanche wasn't really her friend. They were only friends if Blanche had no one better around to have fun with.

Rose hated to have the eyes of strangers always looking at her when she went outside or walked down the street. She missed everything about the farm. She missed having Swiney to play with, even if he was a rough boy sometimes. She missed Blackfoot, and on and on.

"Land sakes, Rose." Mama chuckled. "You'll wear yourself out with all your complainings."

Rose plopped down on Papa's saddle, crossed her arms, and scowled at the floor. Her cares were nothing to make a joke of.

Mama threw the last handful of straw on the floor. Then she came and sat next to Rose, on a crate.

"You know that I don't like to live in a town myself," she said, smoothing her apron with her hands. "When I was not much older than you, I had to go to work in town, sewing up shirts and making buttonholes. I didn't like to be in town, and I didn't like the folks I worked for. I only wanted to stay out on the farm with the family, but it was something that had to be done, to earn money for your aunt Mary to go to school.

"Now we must live in town again, all of us. There's no help for it. What must be done is best done cheerfully."

The blood rushed to Rose's head. If she'd

heard that old saying once, she'd heard it a hundred times. She felt like a baby squalling in the dark, flailing its arms and legs because it had no words to say it was hurting somewhere. "I *won't* be cheerful," she spat out. "I couldn't ever."

Mama's voice went steely. "Mind your tongue, young lady. I won't stand for such freshness. Whatever in the world's gotten into you all of a sudden? I've a mind to . . ."

"Hello! Laura, is that you?" Mrs. Cooley's voice called out from the barn door.

"Why, Emma," Mama sang in her sweetest voice, jumping up to greet her.

"I'm sorry to drop in right out of the blue," Mrs. Cooley said. "But I finally found that bolt of unbleached muslin I told you about. As I was on my way to see Mrs. Rippee, I thought I'd leave off a nice piece you might sew up for curtains. Hello, Rose."

Rose barely looked up as Mama and Mrs. Cooley walked out of the barn, Mama chattering gaily as if nothing had happened.

How could she be like that? Rose grumbled

to herself: vexed one moment, and cheerful the next. It all seemed so unfair. Didn't Mama say she hated living in town? Yet she thought nothing of putting on a beaming, carefree face for others, as if everything were simply perfect.

Rose knew she could never make herself act happy when she wasn't. If that was what it meant to be a grown-up, she would just as soon not become one.

The Arkansas Traveler

It seemed to Rose that Mama had forgotten her tantrum. She never said another word about it.

As soon as Mrs. Cooley left, Abe and Swiney drove up with a wagon full of stove wood. While Mama got dinner ready, Rose helped stack the wood by the back of the house.

From across the tracks she could hear the *slap* of planks being stacked at the lumberyard, and the lowing of cattle at the stock pen near the depot. Shreds of steam like hunks of cotton batting rose into the air from the mill, then disappeared against the leaden autumn sky.

She watched an eastbound local sputter past. The engineer leaned out of his window and waved to them, but Rose had a piece of wood in her hands, and she didn't feel like waving anyway.

"Little girl, you're a-looking mighty puny today," Abe said as he chucked the pieces onto the ground. "I reckon Swiney scared you somethin' bad with that old barrel."

"I guess," Rose said, touching her forehead. "But I'm all right now. It was just a little bump is all."

Abe stood up straight for a moment, took off his hat, and wiped his pale forehead with his kerchief. His deep brown eyes sparkled. "Seems like you could go for some cheerin' up. What you say we tell Rose 'bout the Arkansas Traveler, Swiney-boy?"

"You bet!" Swiney shouted.

"All right, then," said Abe. "Now this here story takes some fiddling to go with it. I ain't got my fiddle with me, but I figure we can make do. Now Swiney, you're a-being the Traveler and I'm a-being the Farmer. Can you recollect the words?"

Swiney nodded his head and looked at Rose with a big grin. "I know it by heart," he said proudly. "Abe's sung it 'bout a hunnert times."

"See now," Abe began, "this here Traveler— that'll be Swiney—was a-riding his horse through the swamps of Arkansas and got himself purely lost." Abe ran his fingers through his thick black hair and sat down on the wagon gate. He took out his plug of tobacco, tore off a piece, and tucked it in his cheek.

Rose slowly took another piece of wood and stacked it on the pile, watching Abe like a hawk. Even Fido sat by the stoop, pricking his ears.

"Now the Traveler come upon a house, an old log house that were a-falling down. The farmer were a-sitting on a barrel in front, and he were old hisself." Then Abe looked at Swiney and winked. "And the Traveler, he called out . . ."

"Hello!" Swiney called out.

"Hello yourself," Abe answered slow as molasses, in a gravelly old man's voice. He climbed down off the wagon gate, perched himself on the woodpile, and lounged back with his hands behind his head and his hat tipped onto his forehead.

"Can you tell me where this road goes?" Swiney piped with a nervous giggle.

"Well, it's ain't moved a step since I been here," Abe answered slowly.

Rose chuckled.

"How long you been living here?" Swiney, the Traveler, asked.

"See the knot on that tree over yonder?" Abe said, pointing lazily. "Waal, it were there when I come, and it's there yet."

"Have you got any spirits?" the Traveler asked.

"Plenty of 'em," the Farmer said. "The missus seen one down by the creek t'other night, and it like to scare her to death."

From the kitchen window, they heard a dish rattle and Mama's laugh.

"I don't mean that kind of spirits. I'm cold, and want some liquor. Have you got any liquor?"

"Had some yesterday," the Farmer said. "And that old cur dog got in the kitchen and licked out the pot."

Now Rose was giggling and Swiney did too.

"You misheard me," he said. "I don't want pot liquor. Have you any whiskey? I'm dry and want some whiskey to drink."

"Oh, whiskey," Abe said, his eyebrows lifting and his head tilting back. "Why, yes, I surely did have some. But that skunk of a boy o' mine, he went and drunk it up."

"I'm hungry, too," Swiney said. "Have you anything to eat?"

"Ain't a bite in the house," Abe said. "Nary mouthful of meat nor speck of cornmeal."

Swiney was laughing now, so much he could hardly get out the words.

"Well . . . well," he giggled, "how far to the next house?"

"Don't know, mister. Ain't never measured."

"Can I leastwise sleep in your house tonight? I will tie my horse to that tree and just go hungry."

Abe winked at Rose. "Roof leaks," he said. "Just one dry place, and me and the missus got to sleep in it. And you cain't tie your horse to that tree, neither. It'd shake the persimmons offen it, and the missus got her eye on 'em for puddin'."

55

"Why don't you fix the leaks?" Swiney asked.

"It's been a-raining of late."

"Why don't you fix 'em when it quits raining?"

"It don't leak then."

Mama laughed loudly and Rose was helpless with giggling. Swiney flapped his arms. "Wait, wait," he said. "There's more."

He looked at Abe, just as Mama came out the back door, smiling and drying her hands on a towel. She sat down on the stoop and rested her arms on her knees.

"Well, I reckon I'll be moving on," Swiney said. "Can you tell me about the road to get out of here?"

"Stranger," Abe said. "You see that gulley over yonder? You got to cross that, then take the big road up the bank. 'Bout a mile on you'll come to a corn patch that's mighty weedy. But don't mind that none. You just keep a-riding.

"'Bout a mile on you'll come to a big boggy swamp. There's a first-rate road some six feet under it.

"Well, 'bout a mile from there, you'll come to where there's two roads. Take the right fork and go 'bout a mile and you'll see it run out. Then come back and take the left fork, and when you get 'most two miles down, you'll come to where there ain't no more road.

"Then you'll be a-thinking yourself mighty lucky iffen you could get back here, where you can stay long as you fancy."

Swiney slapped his knee and whooped. Rose found herself laughing for the first time since they moved, and her heart felt light. It was a relief to let go of her sorrows. Mama rocked back and forth, her laughter echoing from the little barn across the yard.

After they had finished unloading and stacking the stove wood, Abe took his hammer, some nails, and some planks to the little barn and began hammering, fixing a feed trough for Bunting's stall. Rose and Swiney wandered over by the railroad grade. They climbed up on top and looked down the tracks. Fido tagged along, sniffing in the brush for the scent of a mouse or rabbit.

"It's very noisy here," said Rose. "The trains even make the house shake. But Mrs. Cooley said after a while we won't even notice them."

"I wouldn't want to live in town," said Swiney, shying a stone down the tracks. It struck one of the rails with a *ping* and bounced off into the weeds. "I don't like the town boys. Anytime I got to go with Abe to do our tradin', they play tricks and make jokes on me, callin' me piggy boy, on account of my name, and pushin' me in the mud.

"I wish you could of stayed out on the farm, Rose. It's lonesome, and nothin' but babies to play with. It's all Abe wants when he comes in, is playin' with James and Elza."

Rose sighed and looked up and down the row of fenced-in lots that ran along the base of the grade. Behind them, on the south side of the tracks, rose the grain elevator, and next to it the lumberyard with great piles of logs and mounds of sawdust like giant anthills.

In front of them to their right, up the hill, loomed the big schoolhouse, two stories high, with its checkered mansard roof and tall blank windows staring down on the town. School would start soon.

A little tremble ran through Rose. She worried if Blanche would sit with her, and if she would have a teacher she liked. She worried she just couldn't ever manage to fit in anywhere, a town girl now but still wearing her plain gingham and calico dresses, and heavy brogan shoes.

Suddenly, her mind lit up, and she nearly shouted, "I know! You could come to school. Then we could see each other every day."

"School?" Swiney scoffed, hurling another stone down the tracks. Behind them, to the west, a train whistle sounded. Rose spied a man climbing the ladder on the water tower down the tracks by the depot. Number 105, a local, was coming. "What do I need with schoolin'? I never been and I ain't never going."

"I *am* never going. But you might like it," Rose pressed. "If you never went, how can you know? Please, Swiney. Just for a little bit, why don't you come? There's games to play at recess, and at dinnertime you could come home with me."

They had walked a little bit down the track, away from town. Rose looked back. Far down the long glimmering ribbons of track, she saw the bright eye of the locomotive's engine light, and the flag of smoke unfurling above it.

"I *hate* my name," Swiney said suddenly. "I don't want to go to no school and all them boys making a joke on me. Shucks, I could lick any one of 'em," he said savagely. "But all them get together, and nothing to do for it without I get a bad thrashin'."

They sat down on a little hillside above the railroad grade, next to one of the telegraph poles, to wait for the train to come. The wind sang in the wires with a low sighing sound. Swiney took out his pocketknife, cut a switch from a hackberry bush, and began to whittle.

"Is that your real name?" Rose asked. "I never heard of anybody called it before."

"I reckon," Swiney muttered. "It's all I ever was called."

"Maybe it's just a made-up name. Maybe Abe knows," suggested Rose. "He was a big boy when you were born. I bet he remembers why they called you that."

They watched the train wheeze into the station. The long pipe swung out from the water tower, and a cloud of steam billowed out from under the engine, rising up into the cool air and disappearing. People and boxes and wagons swarmed around the train like ants over a fallen apple.

Then the whistle blew, and the chuffing echoed from the hill in front of them.

"Fido!" Rose called out worriedly. An instant later she felt the little black-and-tan spotted terrier's paws on her back, and his cold nose against her neck. She put an arm around him and hugged him close, in case he might get an idea to run across the tracks.

The locomotive rocked gently as it crawled toward them, and they could see the engineer lean out of the cab.

When the train got close, Rose saw the engineer reach over and pull a cord. The whistle blew again. The locomotive lurched screeching down the track, and as it passed right in front of them, the engineer waved his cap and shouted, "Howdy!"

Rose and Swiney waved back, and Fido yipped, struggling to get free of Rose's arm. The freight and passenger cars rattled slowly past. When the train had rolled a little ways beyond them, it started to slow down. Rose spotted a man throwing a shovelful of coal down the embankment from the locomotive. Then a big puff of dark smoke shot into the air, and the train picked up speed again.

Rose didn't like to argue with Swiney about school. She knew how hard it was to be a country-dressed child trying to fit in, but at least no one ever pushed her down in the mud, or snatched her hat to throw it in the privy, as the town boys did to country boys.

"I wish you'd at least try sometime," Rose said. "There are some useful things to learn, and I would like it more than anything if you did."

"Aw, I dunno. Let's go back. Must be near dinner, and I'm hungry as a wolf."

Abe and Swiney's visit changed everything for Rose. Papa came home from delivering a load of feed sacks from the depot to the mill, and the Baird boys shared the pot of fresh hominy and corn bread that Effie had sent with them. Mama fried up salt pork to go along.

They took their first meal in the dining room. It was pleasant to be away from the heat of the cookstove, and to sit as a family again with Abe and Swiney, just as they had in the days before Abe married Effie.

Abe told country brags that kept them all laughing so hard, they could scarcely finish their pie.

"Down Arkansas way, when I was a-growing up with Ma and Pa, Lord rest their souls, the corn grew so darned big, we couldn't burn them cobs for cookwood, on account of they wouldn't no way fit in the stove.

"We had ourselves a purty big fireplace, but the only way to get them cobs in was to saw 'em in half, and then split the chunks into four-foot sticks.

"Yessir, it's the truth. And the dirt on our

place, it were so darn rich that when Ma threwed the corn out for the chickens, they had to catch it in the air or plain starve. Soon's a kernel lit on the ground, it sprouted so quick, the stalk was growed a foot high afore the poor hens could get to it."

Abe's dark eyes gleamed with pleasure as he spoke, and his big, toothy grin seemed to fill the whole room with light. Rose realized that even though she lived in town now, the Bairds were still her dearest friends, good as family. And she was determined to get Swiney to come to school.

Mrs. Rippee's Library

After dinner Abe and Swiney drove back to the farm. When the dishes were washed and dried, Mama said it was high time they returned all the plates, pots, and pie tins that the neighbors had sent their food in.

"Oh, dear," Mama fretted as she laid them all out on the kitchen table. "I don't know as I can remember whose is which. Here, I think this is Mrs. Gaskill's plate. Run over and ask her."

The Gaskills lived next door, the first house to the left if you stood on the Wilders' little porch looking at the street. To the right, across the alley, lived the Hardesty family. There were houses all up and down the other side of the street as well.

Rose had yet to set foot in any neighbor's yard, and she had never needed to introduce herself to strangers. She worried about what she should say to Mrs. Gaskill.

Rose let herself out of their gate and walked along the street to the Gaskills' gate, holding the plate carefully in both hands. The next house beyond on the same side belonged to the McSwains, and after that the street crossed a little bridge over a creek that was so small no one had bothered to give it a name.

On the other side of the creek, far down the street, Rose could see the blacksmith's shop and the pasture beside Hoover's Livery Stable, which was just at the corner of the square in the middle of Mansfield.

Mr. Gaskill was the postmaster, and Jesse Gaskill was a boy in the Fourth Reader with Rose at school. Rose hardly knew Jesse, but he was a good speller and didn't pull the girls' hair or bring grasshoppers to put down their backs.

The Gaskill house was a little bit smaller

than Rose's, liver colored with a wide porch. A row of young sycamore trees that made a kind of fence between the Gaskills' and Rose's houses boasted its fall colors. Bright yellow leaves littered the yard beneath them like shavings of gold.

Rose stood on the sidewalk for a long moment, watching Jesse's little brother and sister building a house out of corncobs on the front steps. Finally she took a deep breath, unlatched the gate, and walked soberly up the path.

The little boy looked up and stared at Rose blankly. The little girl jumped up and ran inside the house, the screen door slamming behind her.

"Mama!" her high-pitched voice shrieked. "Mama! It's a girl here."

Rose heard footsteps inside, and then Mrs. Gaskill came out on the porch, brushing a spot of flour dust from her cheek. The little girl peered out from behind, sucking her thumb and clutching the hem of Mrs. Gaskill's apron with the same hand.

"Well, hello there," she said. "You must be the girl that's moved in next door."

"Yes'm," Rose nearly whispered. "We thank you for the gingerbread cake, and here is your plate back."

"Well, I'm sure you're welcome, dear. It's Rose, isn't it? Such a pretty name.

"But that isn't my plate. Let me have a look at it." She took it and looked closely at the pattern, turning the plate over in her flour-speckled hands. "Yes, I do believe this is Mrs. Hardesty's. I'd recognize those miniature roses anywhere. I'm sure I sent my cake on plain china."

Rose felt herself flush hot with embarrassment. "I'm . . . I'm sorry," she stammered. "I'll come right back."

Rose fled through the gate and up the sidewalk to her own house.

"I feel so foolish," Mama fussed, pulling out Mrs. Gaskill's plain white china plate. "I'd best take these myself. Let's see. I'm sure this pot is Mrs. Robinett's, and these pie tins. Well, how could anyone know? They all look the same."

Mama gathered them all up in a stack. She gave Rose a pale-pink bowl with fluted sides. "I know this had Mrs. Rippee's persimmon pudding. She's the lady that lives straight across the street in the white house. Take it over to her, and remember to say how much Papa liked it. I'll go ask Mrs. Gaskill if she can tell whose of these is which."

The Rippee house sat on a gentle slope of land, close by the street. It was a low house, tucked into the gentle curve of the hillside. It rested more snugly in the ground than other houses did, as if it had grown there.

It was painted snowy white, and so was its picket fence. All along the front lay the frost-burned leaves and dried stems of summer flowers. Moss roses grew by the bricks that edged the path to the porch.

Circles of bricks had been laid in the grass to hold plants and flowers. The one on the left had a prickly low mound of cactus. Mrs. Rippee's hens fluttered in dust baths on the bare ground under the maple tree.

Rose let herself in and walked up to the

porch. A hickory rocking chair sat to one side, and the ceiling was painted sky blue. Rose wished her house had such a big porch. She thought the ceiling was very clever.

The front door was closed, and a lace curtain kept her from seeing in, but Rose could hear noise inside through one of the very tall open windows, and she could smell fresh baking. She knocked very gently and waited. No one came for the longest time. She was just about to knock again when the knob rattled, and the door opened. She jumped in fright.

So did Mrs. Rippee.

Her hand flew to her breast. "My gracious," she said with a laugh. "You startled me, child. How long have you been standing here? Oh, I see you've brought back my bowl. I was just coming out to sweep the porch. I didn't hear you knock."

Mrs. Rippee's pink face smiled at Rose, and the corners of her eyes crinkled kindly behind her glasses. Her silvery hair was parted carefully down the middle and wound into a bun at the back. A starched white apron covered her neat gray dress, and the high lace collar made her look as pretty and pure as an ice flower.

"I believe I scared you more than you scared me," she said, laughing. "Come inside, dear. I just took a baking of bread out of the oven."

"Thank you, ma'am," Rose said. "But I think I ought to be going back. Papa liked the persimmon pudding . . . and so did I," she quickly added.

"Come, come," said Mrs. Rippee, putting a gentle hand on Rose's shoulder and guiding her toward the door. "I'm sure we can find a few minutes to sit and visit. It would be downright unneighborly to send you off just like that. I've got some fresh apple butter from my boy's farm to spread on a nice piece of bread."

Rose followed Mrs. Rippee into the darkness.

"My children are all farmers," she said. "Mr. Rippee is in the practice of law, and he is often away at Hartville.

"I don't get to see my grandchildren much in the summer. They are so busy with chores, and

I do miss the sound of children about the house. Of course, you know all about farming, don't you? Well, character and hard work always go hand in hand, I like to say."

Rose's nostrils filled with the sweet odor of damp earth and yeast. When her eyes could see again, she noticed that all along the tall windows, on the sills and on the floor and in pots on stands, there were plants. Geraniums thick with leaves sprouted brilliant red and pink flowers, and soft ferns with fronds like ostrich feathers hung from hooks in the ceiling. The dark-green leaves of cast-iron plants reached out their eager fingers. Lacy palms swayed gently in the breeze coming in through the window.

"Do you like my plants?" Mrs. Rippee asked.

"Yes ma'am," said Rose. "It's like having a forest in your house. It's very peaceful."

"Gardening is my first love, after Mr. Rippee, of course," she said, beaming as she plucked a yellowing leaf from one of the geraniums. "I got the last of them in off the porch only yesterday; just missed catching the frost.

"Well, come in the kitchen and I'll cut you a nice thick slice of bread. It's a wonderful thing, having farmers in the family. We never want for wholesome, nourishing food.

"I don't like to have my fresh goods from a merchant. They put a big price on, and you can't know where things came from, or how long they've been sitting. Why, my sister once found a mouse's tail in Nelson's butter. Imagine that! Well, it's just as people say; the farmer eats all he can't sell, and the merchant sells what he can't eat."

Mrs. Rippee chattered away the whole while she was cutting the bread, spreading the apple butter, and pouring a glass of milk. Rose sat politely at the kitchen table, listening and watching her move around the kitchen as quick and determined as a little wren.

She thought Mrs. Rippee must be quite lonely. It seemed as if she had so many things to say, as if they all had been bottled up inside of her just waiting for someone to come along and let them out.

Rose liked to listen to her, and she talked to Rose as if she had known her all her life, like a doting aunt or a grandmother.

Just as Rose took her first bite of the still-steaming bread, Mrs. Rippee looked at her with a satisfied smile and said, "Listen to me, prattling like a guinea hen. Now here you are, living in town. How do you find it?"

Rose hurriedly swallowed. "It's very nice. But I miss living at Rocky Ridge. That's our farm."

"Of course you do," Mrs. Rippee said eagerly. "I'll tell you something: I grew up on a farm and I never wanted to leave, but Mr. Rippee wouldn't hear of it. Said it was plain foolishness, him off getting up lawsuits at the courthouse in Hartville and me left behind to manage by myself. So we took this place in town, and we've been here ever since.

"Just between you and me," she said, leaning forward and winking, "it's Mr. Rippee didn't want to live so far from town. He likes to go to the hotel, smoke his cigars, and hear the latest news from the traveling men and the politicians. Men think we don't see things, but we women are a lot smarter than we ever let on."

Rose warmed right up to old Mrs. Rippee. She was always respectful to her elders. She knew she must never interrupt them, never disagree with anything they said. She must be polite when they looked at her. Politely, when asked, she must tell her name, her age, and say, Yes ma'am, I like school, and Yes ma'am, I obey my kind teachers.

When their talk was so boring that she ached all over, she sat still, being seen and not heard. Then, if they began to say anything interesting, Mama sent Rose out to play.

Mrs. Rippee was not like those other old people. It seemed as if she wanted to be Rose's friend, and that drew Rose to her like a warm, gentle hug.

"Now you must tell me, what is it that interests you? Do you like to cook? Are you working on your first quilt yet?"

Rose thought a moment. "I like to help Mama with the cooking. I sew, but not so well. I am very fond of reading."

"Are you?" Mrs. Rippee said, setting a

second slice of bread on Rose's plate. "What have you read?"

Rose was staggered. Books were a special private world all her own, and she was proud of her reading. No one she knew, not even grown-ups, read as much as she, but no one outside her own family had ever asked her what books she liked to read.

In her confusion, Rose tried to remember the books she would not be embarrassed to say she'd read. Some of them were grown-up books, and she didn't want to seem as if she were boasting.

"*Five Little Peppers, and How They Grew*; *Five Little Peppers Grown Up*; *Afloat in the Forest*. I read those. I am fond of poetry as well. Mama has a book of poems by Mr. Alfred, Lord Tennyson. It has a poem I have read many times: 'The Charge of the Light Brigade.' "

"My, my," Mrs. Rippee said. "That *is* a stirring poem. *Into the valley of death rode the six hundred*. Mr. Rippee and I have a great many volumes we have collected over the years. You know, this house used to be the school in town before they built the big one on the hill. One of the things I like best about this place is the bookshelves. Come and see."

In Mrs. Rippee's jungly parlor, all along one wall, and even around the corner on the other wall, were shelves and shelves of books, more books than Rose had ever seen or ever thought there could be in the whole world.

The shelves had great glass doors on them, and shiny brass locks to keep them closed. One whole end of that room gleamed with nothing but books, from the floor to higher than Rose's head. There were two small shelves of books in the Fourth Reader room at school, but all those books together couldn't fill a single shelf of Mrs. Rippee's.

Rose liked nothing better than the feel of a book in her hands, the musty smell when she opened it, the cool rich weave of the cloth covers, and the perfect rows of words printed on crisp, clean paper. Now rows and rows of books, with gold and silver words on the bindings, and dark covers in red and brown and black and green, beckoned to her, begged her to reach out and touch them, to know their secrets.

For the longest moment, she could only stare in speechless awe, hardly hearing a word Mrs. Rippee said.

" . . . when Mr. Rippee and I first were married, of course. I've read every one, and some more than once. A good book is the best of friends, the same today and forever. Why don't you have a look?"

"May I?" Rose breathed.

"Why, of course," Mrs. Rippee said with pleasure. She took a key from her workbasket, which sat on the floor by the davenport, and unlocked each of the glass doors with a little rattling sound.

Rose was overwhelmed. It seemed the whole wide world that she knew nothing about was there, right in front of her.

She approached those shelves as solemnly as she might enter a hushed church. She reached out her hand and touched the binding of one book, then let her fingers drag lightly down the row, feeling the engraved lettering, until she stopped at an interesting title: *The Innocents Abroad*, by Mark Twain.

"You may look at it, if you like," Mrs. Rippee said. "It is a very lively report of a man's journey to Europe. A little bit shocking, some might say, but I found it quite amusing."

Rose pulled it out and felt the weight of it in her palm. She carefully let it fall open in her hands.

Her eyes pounced hungrily into the middle of a paragraph. *How many priests have ye on hand?* she read.

> *"The day's results are meager, good my*
> *lord. An abbot and a dozen beggarly friars is*
> *all we have."*
> *"Hell and furies! Is the estate going to*
> *seed? Send hither the mountebanks.*
> *Afterward, broil them with the priests."*

Rose guffawed, then glanced furtively at Mrs. Rippee. She'd never read anything so wicked. She quickly closed the book and slipped it back into its place on the shelf.

"Some people think Mr. Twain a rascal for the things he writes." Mrs. Rippee picked up the feather duster she kept hanging from a hook at the end of the bookshelves and flicked it at the bindings.

"I suppose it isn't suitable for one so young, but there are many other books I believe your mother would find very improving. Why don't we pick one, and I can ask her? Then, if she approves, you may borrow it."

Just then the kitchen clock began to chime.

As the fourth *gong* faded away, Rose gasped. "Oh," she groaned. "I just know Mama will be waiting for me, and I ought to be getting the stove wood in for supper.

"Thank you so much, so very much. It was very nice."

"Of course, dear. But you must come back. Anytime at all."

"Oh, I will. I honestly will," Rose blurted.

Gold Rush!

When Rose came out of Mrs. Rippee's yard, the sight of Mama standing on the porch of the Hardesty house, talking to Mrs. Hardesty, comforted her. Mama wouldn't scold her for taking so long; she herself still had to start her evening chores.

Rose was glad to find Fido patiently waiting for her on the gravel sidewalk. His little tail wagged furiously, and he barked twice to let her know he didn't like to be left alone for such a long time.

Rose raced Fido home, across the street, down the alley, and through the gate of the barn lot. She gathered kindling from the wood-pile, stuffed it hurriedly into the stove, and lit the fire. Then she dashed back outside and pumped two buckets of water from the well.

It was a pleasure to fetch water at the town house. She only had to pump the handle a few times, and all the clean, fresh water they could ever want came gushing out the spout.

On the farm, she'd had to carry the bucket to the spring in the gully behind the house, dip it in, and sometimes, when the spring ran low in dry weather, top it off with the gourd dipper. In the winter she had to break the ice, and her hands stung from the cold water. Then she must climb the steep path lugging the heavy, sloshing bucket to the house or the barn, and go all the way back for another and another and another until she thought her arm would pull right off.

Now getting water was easy, and they needed fewer bucketsful. Papa kept the horses stabled with the freight wagon at Hoover's Livery, and the mules lived on the farm, where Abe and Swiney took care of them.

All the while she worked, Rose's feet never seemed to touch the ground, and she found herself chuckling at the sight of Mrs. Gaskill's little girl, sitting on her heels in their backyard, petting a hen on its head and talking to it.

The dusky sun peeked through a hole in a bank of clouds, setting the sky aflame with brilliant streaks of colored light that seemed to be trying to pull themselves together into a rainbow. A yelping flight of geese heading south in the fading light sounded like laughter to her.

Broil the priests, she thought as she pumped. The idea sent a shiver up her spine. It couldn't be true that anyone would do such a thing. Mrs. Rippee had said that book was amusing. It had to be just a made-up story, Rose decided with relief.

Mama finally came home with a big grin on her face. She didn't say a word about how long Rose had taken to return Mrs. Rippee's bowl. Mama herself had too much to talk about, as they worked together in the kitchen getting supper ready.

"I *like* Mrs. Helfinstine," she said brightly.

"We had a visit as lively as I can remember having with anyone. She told me all about her grandfather coming west in an ox-drawn wagon from Tennessee before the war. And I told her about growing up on the prairie.

"It is interesting to see how other folks keep their houses. Some of them are simply beautiful, and neat as pins. And some . . . Well, I'm not one to gossip. I guess I learned some things about the folks in town," she said mysteriously.

"Oh, and can you imagine? Mrs. Helfinstine may even put me up for the Eastern Star."

"What's that?" Rose asked, peeling potatoes at the table. The kitchen, with its steaming pots and sizzling meat, smelled pleasantly of home.

"It's a women's charitable society, for the wives of Masons. You know that Papa is a Mason."

"He is? What's a Mason?"

"Well, I'm not exactly sure. They keep certain secrets among themselves. But it is an ancient men's society, the Free and Accepted Masons.

"I think it would be wonderfully uplifting, to be taken into the Order of the Eastern Star. They work to improve the town, and help the needy. Your aunt Carrie is a Worthy Matron of the Eastern Star, back in South Dakota.

"Some of the ladies want to petition the merchants to put in a resting room for the farmwives, for when they come to town. It's a sin and a shame the way they—we—have to sit out on a hard wagon seat in rain and snow while the husbands lounge about inside doing their trading. And the nearest privy is all the way to the edge of town, at the school."

Rose wanted to know more about Worthy Matrons and Free and Accepted Masons, but she couldn't get a word in edgewise. Then Papa came home, and supper was never livelier.

"And the Robinetts have such a pretty white house, with German siding," Mama gushed. "And that clever turret on the top. They have a hired girl. Imagine that! Paying out good money every week, not to mention what she must eat, just to have another woman underfoot 'til you can't call your soul your own.

"I wouldn't have a hired girl, not if you paid me for it. When I want to speak to my husband for his own good, I wouldn't have a stranger sitting there gawping. I don't know how Mrs. Robinett stands it."

Papa laughed as he dished himself another helping of kraut. "Bess, you ought to save a bit of breath to cool your coffee."

Mama chuckled and sat back in her chair. "It's true. I'm chattering like a sparrow. I don't know what's gotten into me. I feel just so . . . frisky of a sudden."

Rose was bursting to tell Mama and Papa about Mrs. Rippee and her shelves of books when Papa scraped his chair back and got up to pour the coffee.

"You might like to hear what's going on uptown," he said. "I saw Deaver at the depot, all packed with a carpetbag boarding the Stockman's Special. The bank foreclosed him off his farm after the drought killed his crops.

"He's sold off his animals and sent his wife and boy to stay with her sister down in Ava. Says he won't be back 'til spring."

"Where's he going?" Mama asked.

"The Klondike River, in Yukon Territory, to hunt for gold."

"The Yukon!" Mama gasped. "Why, that's the end of the earth."

"Some folks think it's the pot at the end of the rainbow," said Papa. "Seems a farmer from Seymour just got back. They say he brought home fifteen thousand dollars he made in gold nuggets, some of 'em just lying out right on top of the ground, in plain sight."

Mama's mouth gaped open and she shook her head in wonderment. "Fifteen thousand dollars!" she said. "A whole lifetime of farming couldn't earn so much."

"Whole town's jabbering about it," Papa said. "There were some young fellows down at the depot today, talking about going up there themselves. Railroad's put out a special poster, hawking tickets."

"Where's Yukon Territory?" Rose wanted to know.

Papa moved his plate aside and drew a map on the red-and-white-checkered tablecloth with his finger. "Here we are, in Missouri," he said. "Out west is California and the Pacific Ocean. Up the coast, way up here, is the Yukon. There's a gold rush on up there, along the Klondike River; thousands of men digging in the hills trying to get rich. And plenty of 'em doing just that, too.

"I read in the newspaper where a boat got back from up there with sixty men on it, every one of 'em wealthy from gold. I tell you, Bess, if I was a few years younger . . ."

"Humpf!" Mama interrupted. "If you were a few years younger, I'd still say dreams come true for those who wake up and put in an honest day's work. To think of poor Mrs. Deaver spending the winter worrying herself sick.

"I guess I can read a newspaper same as anyone, Manly. That's rough country up there, full of desperadoes and ne'er-do-wells."

"Don't forget, your pa did the very same thing," said Papa, lighting his pipe. "The prairie was a rough place when your folks settled there."

"Maybe so," Mama said. "But we were farmers, not fortune seekers. Any man that gets a notion to run off and leave his family just so's he can try to get rich looking for gold ought to be using his head for something besides a hat rack."

The next day after church Mrs. Cooley came to Sunday dinner with Paul and George. Papa went to pick them up in the wagon so he could bring back a chifforobe that Mrs. Cooley was giving to Mama. It had beautiful wooden scrollwork and brass handles on five whole drawers for folded clothes. It even had a closet for hanging things. On the inside of the closet door hung a long mirror with beveled edges.

The chifforobe had been where Mr. Cooley kept his clothing, and Mrs. Cooley said it was high time she put the past in the past.

"We don't need it anymore, and my bedroom has a nice closet. Besides, it's so small there's hardly room for the bed."

She also gave Papa some of Mr. Cooley's shirts, and one of his good suits. The rest she would keep for Paul, when he was big enough to wear them.

After dinner Mama, Papa, and Mrs. Cooley sat around the table talking over their coffee. Rose and the Cooley boys put on their coats and went outside.

A blowing wind had chased away the clouds, and the sun shone bright and warm. Tumbling leaves danced in the air like butterflies and huddled in piles against the fences and around the tree trunks.

From around the neighborhood came the high, light voices of children playing. Mrs. Gaskill opened her kitchen door and threw a ham bone out to their dog.

"Let's walk uptown," said Paul. "I want to see what the news is at the depot."

"What news?" Rose asked. George picked a stick up off the ground and played tug-of-war with Fido.

"Any news," Paul said. "There's always something coming over the telegraph. Come on."

"I'm not sure," said Rose. "Mama said it was no place for a girl to play."

"Aw, that's a lot of stuffing. It's just an old depot, is all. Lots of the folks walk uptown. Besides, it's Sunday. There's hardly anybody out and about."

They let themselves out of the gate into the alley that ran between Rose's house and the Hardestys'. Then they walked around the back of the barn lot and down the muddy lane that ran along the base of the railroad grade toward the depot.

The whole time Rose's ears were pricked for Mama's voice, and she glanced furtively back, to see if Mama might come out of the kitchen. Finally, when they had passed behind the Gaskills' and out of sight of her own house, Rose breathed a nervous little sigh of relief.

"See those wires up there?" Paul said. "Just about every minute there's some message going over them, from depot to depot, all the way across the country. Important messages about train schedules, and freight orders. And lots of messages are just for plain folks, telling them about family news, and drummers wiring for hotel rooms."

Rose had heard of drummers but she had never actually seen one. A drummer was a man who traveled the country selling things, drumming up business.

Rose looked at the wires that were strung from the telegraph poles all along the tracks.

"How does it do that?" she wanted to know. "How could words go through those little ropes?"

"They aren't ropes," George piped. "They're wires, made of metal. Right, Paul?"

"It's electricity," Paul said. "'Member when I showed you about Morse code, dots and dashes? Well, electricity makes a little spark, like a tiny bit of lightning. And each spark is a dot or a dash, and all those dots and dashes make words."

At the bridge over the little creek they stopped to race sticks in the water.

"Is the telegraph like a telephone?" The town was strung with telephone poles and wires. Blanche's house had a telephone, but Mama said she wouldn't have one. She said she had nothing so important to say that it couldn't wait until she walked across town.

"Naw," said Paul. "A telephone works on electricity too, but some way that gets it to carry your own voice. I don't know how it works, exactly, but it's different from telegraphing. And you can't talk to anybody that isn't in your own town. A telegraph message can go around the world."

Rose was bewildered about electricity. She couldn't imagine how words and voices could be turned into bits of lightning and squeezed through those thin wires.

Electric lights were just as big a mystery. Blanche had told her about all the lights she saw when her family went to the Chicago World's Fair: thousands of electric arc lights, and a giant Ferris wheel just covered with them, Blanche had said. Electricity captured the sun and held it shining into the night, and somehow electricity could burn without making a flame, or causing smoke.

None of it made a shred of sense to Rose.

They passed behind the blacksmith shop, and across from the saloon they stepped up onto the empty depot platform. Rose had been there twice before, when Mr. Cooley's body came home, and again to see Grandma and Grandpa Wilder off to Louisiana after their visit the past summer.

This was the first time she'd been without Mama and Papa, and she felt as if she were on some terribly wicked adventure. She was glad there was no one waiting on the benches to see her.

Paul and George strode confidently down the brick platform toward the depot building. Rose hung back, unsure what to do.

When Paul and George stopped at a window in the depot, Rose hurried to catch up. Paul leaned on the sill, talking to someone inside.

"Hey there, Paul," a man's hearty voice called out. "What're you boys up to today? Gonna buy you some tickets to the Yukon?"

"Yeah!" George cried out. "We're gonna go get rich digging gold. Just you wait 'n' see."

"Aw, shut up!" Paul scolded. "You aren't going anywhere. Hey, Mr. Nickles. Whatcha hear on the wire?"

"Mighty quiet today," Mr. Nickles said.

"Number Five got a hotbox just east of Ash Grove. She's runnin' fifteen minutes late. They say there's a bad storm down in the Gulf of Mexico. Don't know if it's comin' our way, but it washed out plenty of track down there."

Listening to the easy way Paul talked to Mr. Nickles, and seeing the carefree manner of his lanky body lounging against the windowsill, his hat pushed back a little, Rose realized that Paul was practically a grown-up man now. His voice was nearly as deep as a man's, and he had a shadow of downy mustache on his upper lip.

He was working now, helping Papa with the draywagon, and sometimes he earned extra money to help with the household expenses unloading freight from the trains. Paul was so good, taking care of his mother and George. Rose's heart ached just thinking of it.

Even before Mr. Cooley died, Paul had started to learn telegraphy. When he finished school in two years, he had told Rose in his most earnest voice, he might even work at the depot, sending and receiving those important messages.

Especially since his father died, Paul had shed the last of his boyishness. He was almost fourteen years old now, tall and handsome. He smiled less, and there were moments when Rose was talking to him that she could see in his dark, sober eyes that his thoughts had drifted off on a faraway ocean.

She had always loved Paul as a brother, but suddenly she looked at him with a special tenderness that gathered in her chest, like an embrace, and radiated a thrill along all her nerves. She took a deep breath to calm herself.

The empty depot was still, except for the voices of Paul and Mr. Nickles, the clicking of the telegraph key in the office, and the low moan of the wind in the wires.

Paul called out the words as the key clattered away. "Eastbound local number One-oh-five, three twenty, on time from West Plains."

Rose was curious to see what the telegraph key looked like, but she was too shy to peer in. She walked over to the curb and stared down the tracks.

In the hushed quiet of a Sunday afternoon,

the depot waited. Down the tracks a dog hopped over the rails and padded off into the weeds. Bits of paper and leaves blew about where a thundering engine would come rocking and panting into the depot. People would swarm over the platform, calling out to each other in urgent, hurried voices. The freight wagons stood empty, their handles flipped up and resting in the air, waiting for trunks and boxes and barrels to be piled on them and carted away.

The long, empty platform echoed with the memory of trains Rose had seen there, of Mr. Cooley's wooden coffin being unloaded, and of Grandma tearfully waving her handkerchief from the window of a passenger car. From the very place where Rose stood, Mr. Deaver had gone off to seek his fortune on the Klondike River. From here, a person could go anywhere in the world, and maybe come back rich.

The depot was a place where important things happened, and could happen, any time of day, or even in the middle of the night. Mr. Nickles and the other station agents were the only people awake in all of Mansfield while the rest of the town slept.

In between, the depot sat there, patiently waiting, lonely and windswept.

She noticed a door to her right with a sign on it: Waiting Room—Whites Only. To the left of the open window was another opening with no door that led into a small dark room. It had a sign, too: Colored.

Farther down the platform, the depot had other rooms marked Freight and Express. Rose peeked around the corner of the depot at the town square, just as Paul called out, "Hey, Rose! C'mon. We'd best be getting back."

As they walked home, Rose wanted to know about the signs. "Why do they have different rooms for white clothes and colored?" she asked. "What's the difference what people are wearing?"

Paul burst out laughing, and an instant later, so did George, when he realized the joke.

"Haven't you ever seen any colored folks?" Paul said. "Those signs tell 'em where they're supposed to wait. Whites in the big room, colored in the little one."

Rose was shocked, and she blushed at her foolishness. She had seen Negroes only once or twice, in towns along the way on the long wagon trip from South Dakota. But never in Mansfield.

"Why do they have to wait in different rooms?"

"Dunno," Paul said. "They just do. Every depot has different rooms."

Rose shook her head. She was baffled by so many things—electricity, telephones, the telegraph—and now the different waiting rooms.

Sometimes it seemed the more she knew, the less she understood.

Settling In

The next weeks flew by, and hardly a day passed without some visitor coming to the house.

There were so many traveling men that Mama was almost afraid to answer the door. They came in their fine suits, starched collars, and derby hats, carrying big leather sacks. They tried to sell Mama books, magazine subscriptions, tin goods, knives and scissors, and even lightning rods. But Mama would buy nothing from a drummer. She said she could find everything she needed in town. She tried always to be polite, but sometimes it was very difficult.

"Lightning rods," she laughed. "Whatever for?"

"To carry the lightning away from your house, ma'am," the traveling man said, stepping up onto the sill. He fumbled in his bag and pulled out a pamphlet. "I don't like to scare folks, but the truth's the truth, to the end of reckoning. You've got a fine house here, I'd say the finest in this town that I've seen yet.

"It only takes a single strike to set a place on fire. It's the thunder that frights, but the lightning that smites."

"Yes, well, I don't think . . ." Mama tried to interrupt.

"You know this is country favored by lightning, as it sits on a high plateau, close to the clouds. Our company has gone to great expense to employ the counsel of a respected university professor who has studied the question. No doubt about it, this is a most dangerous problem here in the Ozarks.

"Now I've seen what lightning can do, ma'am. You wouldn't like your family—I see you have a beautiful little girl there—you wouldn't want her to be unprepared and unprotected, would you?"

"We are well enough prepared, thank you," Mama said. She tried to ease the door closed, but the traveling man wouldn't budge.

"Now, I understand, ma'am." He began talking very quickly. "This is a thing you might not have considered. But if you will permit me to explain our system—very simple, really, and only the finest materials money can buy. At a very low cost, a special price that we offer only to folks in your area. When you consider what it would take to replace this fine home, I'm sure you'll agree that such a small investment . . ."

Mama gently pushed the door shut. The lightning rod man stumbled backward to get his nose out of the way.

"Think it over," his muffled voice called out. "I'm here for just a few days, and our special offer is good only 'til then." An instant later the pamphlet slid under the door.

"Really!" Mama said, rolling her eyes. "I've never seen such boldness. That's the first time I ever had to close a door in someone's face."

Every so often a tramp knocked at the back door for work. There were no chores that Papa couldn't take care of himself, but Mama always gave a cold boiled potato or a piece of corn bread.

One day when Rose and Mama were getting dinner, Mama yelped in surprise when a man's ragged face appeared in the kitchen window. There was a knock on the door and Mama opened it, just a crack.

"I'm shorely sorry to trouble you, ma'am," his gravelly voice said. "Could you kind folks be a-sparing a bite of food for a poor fella what ain't had no work in quite a spell?"

"Well, I . . . I suppose," said Mama. "Just you wait there a minute."

Mama closed the door and looked at Rose, her brow furrowed doubtfully. Rose strained to see out the window. The man stood with his hands in his pants pockets. He had no coat, and one of his galluses was torn. His shoes were wrapped in rags, and he stamped his feet to stay warm.

"Come away from that window," Mama whispered. "It's rude to stare."

"Mama, he's cold. Shouldn't we let him in to warm?"

Mama drew the curtains over the window, then peeked out through a little space between them. "Papa will be home anytime. We'll wait for him. I don't like to have a stranger in the house when we are by ourselves."

When Papa came home, he invited the tramp inside.

"It's only Asa Combs," he told Mama, setting a chair by the stove for Asa to sit in. "Asa, I thought you'd be in California by now."

"Well sir, I got as fur as Kansas City and run out of money." He held his hands out to soak up the heat. Then he choked out a gurgling chuckle and wiped a squinty eye with the back of his hand. "I'll tell you the truth, Mr. Wilder. It ain't money I run out of, it were the brains God gave a dumb chicken. I lost most of it in a saloon, and the rest got stole offen me whilst I was a-sleeping it off.

"Well, bein's they ain't no gold in Kansas

City, I hopped a freight and come back. But they ain't nary jobs hereabouts, what with the bad crops and all. I reckon I'm up agin it this winter."

"You just come and sit with us and have some dinner," said Papa. "After we eat, I'll take you uptown. The folks who bought the Mansfield Hotel were telling me just this morning that they need a handyman around the place. Comes with a room and board, too."

Mr. Combs sat to dinner stoop-shouldered and stared hungrily at the pot of beans and the dish piled with steaming boiled potatoes and onions. Mama spooned up Mr. Combs' plate first, but he waited until everyone had been served. The instant Papa picked up his fork, Mr. Combs dove in.

He ate and ate and ate. When he had finished, he wiped his plate so clean with his corn bread that it shone. Then he pushed his chair back, and Papa said, "You aren't full already, are you Asa? Have a little more."

Mama dished up another plateful, and he polished that right off. When he needed to clean his mouth, he pulled out an old, crumpled page of a magazine from his pocket and wiped his face, the paper rasping against his stubbly beard.

Mr. Combs hardly spoke at all. He couldn't; his mouth was always full. Papa said later that both his legs must have been hollow. That afternoon, he took Mr. Combs down to the hotel. By suppertime he had a bath, clean clothes, and his own room.

"Makes a body feel proud to help an old fellow like that out," Papa said. "Asa's an old-timer from here, not like those drifters that camp along the railroad tracks, stealing and making trouble. He'll do just fine, so long's he stays away from the saloon."

Mrs. Helfinstine often dropped in to exchange receipts with Mama and to sit in the kitchen over cups of tea, trading stories of their families and childhoods. Mrs. Gaskill was always calling over the fence to ask if Rose or Mama had seen her little girl, Ivy, or her little boy, John.

One day two ladies from the Order of the Eastern Star came to talk to Mama about putting her up for membership. Mama spent all morning cleaning, and pressing her best dress. She rushed about the house and snapped at Rose to hurry and finish her chores.

Mama arranged the willowware cups and saucers on the freshly ironed tablecloth, and put out a platter of gingerbread she had baked the night before.

When they finally arrived, Mama sent Rose outside to feed and water the chickens. They had already been fed and watered, so Rose went to visit Mrs. Rippee, and borrowed a book about the Roman Empire, which she sat reading in the warmth of the little barn.

A few days later Mrs. Cooley came to help Mama and Rose make curtains for nearly all the windows. On the farm Mama liked to keep her windows uncovered. She always said they were the prettiest pictures, changing every hour of the day. But the town house could be seen into from every side, and they must have their privacy.

They made the curtains from old sheets and scraps of dress goods. Now that Papa was hauling goods all over town, he sometimes brought home bolt ends from Reynolds' and Nelson's that weren't long enough to sell for dress goods.

"They aren't fancy. I'd love to have lace, but at least the house feels more cozy now," Mama said when they had hung curtains in the empty parlor and the two extra bedrooms.

Papa was busy almost all the time. When he wasn't hauling goods to and from the depot, he worked for Mr. Waters delivering coal oil. Sometimes he would be gone all day on a trip to Hartville, the county seat that was ten miles to the north, or south to Ava.

Sometimes he helped people move. When he did, he almost always brought home something those people didn't need or wanted to sell for a low price. One day he brought home a carpet, in a pink rose design.

"Why, it's practically brand-new," Mama said excitedly when they rolled it out in the parlor. "Just needs a good beating, is all. And I can just whipstitch that frayed corner, and no one will ever know the difference."

"You wouldn't believe some of the things people give away or sell off for a song," said Papa. "We're going to do just fine here, Bess. Buying Cooley's drayage business was the best decision we ever made. The money's good, and the opportunities come along every day."

In no time at all they had beds for both of the extra rooms, and night tables, and dressers, even. All of those came from the Mansfield Hotel, when Papa helped move in new furniture for the guest rooms.

One day Papa brought home a hall tree where he could hang his good hat and Mama could sit to put on her shoes and check herself in the mirror before she went out. One of the legs was broken, but Papa fixed it one night so that it was good as new. Rose could hardly tell where it had been repaired.

He brought an oak jardinier table for the parlor with spindles all around and fancy scroll-work rungs. Mama set the family Bible on it, with a leaf of Bible plant sticking out from the pages to keep away the bugs that might bore holes in the pages.

Then one day Papa strode into the kitchen with a grin on his face.

"Come with me," he said simply to Mama.

"What is it, Manly?"

"Just come with me."

Mama looked at him suspiciously for a moment. Then she put the iron down on the stove, and Rose followed her through the dining room and the parlor to the front porch.

There at the front gate stood the draywagon; Paul was tying the team to the hitching rail. The wagon was full of something bulky, with a cloth thrown over it.

Papa walked to the wagon, and Paul helped him throw back the cloth. Under it was a whole suite of parlor furniture.

"Oh, Manly!" Mama cried out. She dashed down the walk to see better.

"It's a complete set," said Papa, rubbing his cold hands together. "Brand spanking new."

Mama looked in the back of the wagon, her hand to her mouth, her eyes wide with disbelief. It was real parlor furniture, with a davenport that Papa called a tête-à-tête, a rocker, an easy chair, and an armless parlor chair. Every piece was covered in a beautiful bottle-green tapestry with yellow and pink flowers all over.

"Land sakes," Mama exclaimed, hugging herself against the cold. Her breath came in rapid puffs of steam. "But how . . . Nobody could give this away, Manly."

"Darn near," Papa boasted. "Some fella in town ordered it from Garve Beckham at the Furniture Emporium. When it came in, he didn't have the money, and Beckham just wanted to be rid of it. He took half the price, just twelve dollars."

Mama's eyes flashed. "Since when do we have twelve dollars to throw away? I hadn't noticed that money started growing on trees."

"Just about," said Papa, opening the tailgate. "Paul, give a hand here, son. I traded stove wood for it."

Mama's face relaxed into a broad smile. "Oh,

it's just too good to be true. Hurry and get them inside, for heaven's sake. It looks like it might rain any minute."

Mama fluttered about the parlor and looked out the front door like a mother cat worried about her kittens. Papa and Paul brought in the easy chair first. When they had set it down where she wanted it, Mama ran her hand over the fabric, picked off the bits of lint, and untangled the worsted black fringe that hung all around the bottom like the hem of a gown.

"Look," she purred. "There's even a gold tassel on the front of each arm."

She turned it a little bit this way, then a little bit that way, and her eyes darted about the room, thinking where to put the next piece.

Rose couldn't wait to sit in it. She plopped down, and bounced herself on the springy seat. She ran her hands over the nubby embroidered fabric, and looked closely at the fine colored threads that had been cleverly woven into leaves and stems and blossoms. Her hand lifted the tassel, and she let the ropy threads slip between her fingers like water.

That was a grand chair to sit in. Rose felt like a queen on her throne, with its high sculpted back, big plush arms, and the delicate hem that fluttered in the breeze coming through the open door, and . . .

"Rose, come up off there this instant," Mama scolded. "In your work dress and greasy apron! This is parlor furniture, not for lying about in your everydays."

She jumped up, and Mama quickly brushed off the seat with her hand. But Rose was too excited to mind being scolded.

Finally all the pieces were in the room, and Mama stood at the doorway looking and shaking her head in amazement. Papa stood next to her, hands on his hips, proud as a rooster.

The room looked so graceful and serene. It was a real parlor now.

"Mama, we should have some plants," Rose suggested. "Mrs. Rippee has so many in her parlor, it's like a forest."

"Yes, and some nice lace antimacassars and . . . it's just . . . more than I ever dreamed," Mama bubbled. "And so soon after moving in.

Who would have thought? It's just lovely, Manly. Thank you so much."

She surprised Papa with a kiss on his cheek. He chuckled, and Paul caught Rose's eyes for an instant, then looked away bashfully.

Papa walked over and sat down in the easy chair, stretched his legs, and sighed happily. Rose clapped a hand over her mouth to keep from giggling.

"Manly Wilder!" Mama rebuked. "In your dirty overalls!"

"Balderdash," said Papa. "I can sit in my own chair if I want. That's what the durn thing's for."

"Well, at least let me throw a cloth over it," Mama said, rushing back to the bedroom to find an old sheet. "I declare," her voice echoed through the dining room. "You'd think I was living with a tribe of heathens."

Papa looked at Rose with twinkling eyes and winked, and they all had a hearty laugh, even Paul. Rose thought he never looked so handsome as when he smiled.

Call Me Nate

Out on the farms the harvest season finally ended. That summer's drought had hurt everyone. The orchards bore late; Papa said the apples came in smaller and not as sweet as they should be. Then a bad storm knocked most of them off the trees before they could be picked. Bruised falls wouldn't keep for shipping, and shipped apples always brought the best prices.

"At least we weren't counting on our own apples this year," Papa said. "That's something to be grateful about."

The corn harvest came in thin, and the dry

weather had killed the second crop of hay. Corn and hay had to be brought in by railroad from other places, and the price was so high, many farmers could hardly pay to feed their stock. But now that Papa was working in town, their own animals would have enough to eat.

There were still hogs to be butchered, although they rendered greasy because they had fed on grass and roots for too long, and there wasn't corn enough to firm them up.

On a frosty November day with gusting flurries of snow to add an extra sting to the grayness, Rose, Mama, and Papa all went to the Stubbinses' farm to help with the hateful chores of grinding sausage and cubing up fat and stirring the smoky lard kettle.

Rose and Alva worked together, with the other women, but Rose could hardly think of a thing to say to Alva. The many times they had played together, exploring the woods or trying to course bees or walking along the railroad tracks, were all in the past. Rose was a town girl now, and Alva was still a country girl who would rather milk cows and help with the haying than go to school or read a book.

As she huddled against the cold and wiped away tears brought by the smoke from the lard fire, Rose realized that she and Alva were as different now as horses and dogs. Something had changed. In fact, everything was always changing.

When she was a little girl, she thought she would always live on the prairie with Mama and Papa, and visit her grandma and grandpa Ingalls and her aunts anytime she wished. Now they had moved for the fifth time in her life, into a new house with new neighbors, far away from South Dakota.

Rose had thought that Blanche was her best friend, but now she wasn't sure about that. Mr. Cooley had died. Paul was growing into a man. Nothing could ever stay the same.

Something about that gave Rose a twinge of sadness, but it excited her at the same time because she was changing, too. She would be eleven years old soon. She could cook a meal by herself and handle Papa's team when he needed help. And she was old enough to wonder what it might be like to be in love.

She realized that she had been thinking of Paul more and more, about where he was and what he was doing, and feeling a bit shy when he was around. That was a hazy feeling, a yearning without knowing what she yearned for, thrilling and uncomfortable at the same time.

That feeling came from the deepest, most secret part of her, and it was something she could never talk about with anyone.

One Sunday, the Wilders went to Rocky Ridge for dinner with the Bairds. James and Elza were crawling now, and Rose spent nearly every moment before dinner holding them, making faces for them, and helping feed them their scraped apple and cornmush.

After dinner she and Swiney went out to the barn to look at the mules, and then for a walk in the orchard. It was a good feeling to be on their land again, and to see how much the apple trees had grown since Papa had planted them three years ago. The orchard was filling in, except here and there where Abe had chopped down the trees that were hurt by the cyclone.

The forest that had been burned over by the fire that summer looked even more forlorn than Rose remembered. The blackened skeletons of the trees seemed to be crying out in sorrow against the low, dirty clouds. The forest floor was bare and muddy with ash dust. Those woods reminded Rose of a graveyard.

"School takes up tomorrow," Rose said as she peeled a bit of burned bark off the trunk of a tall hickory tree. "You could come. I just bet we'd be in the same Reader."

"I already told you," said Swiney. "I don't want to get in no fights with those town boys."

"You mean because of your name? Did you ask Abe about it? Did you ask him if Swiney's your real name?"

Swiney's eyes flickered with excitement. "Gosh, I plumb forgot." Then he kicked at a stone on the ground. "Aw, it wouldn't make no difference."

"Any difference," Rose corrected.

"Any difference. I'm still a country jake. They wouldn't let me play with them any-ways."

"Of course they would," Rose insisted. "There's George Cooley; he's your same age and he would play with you. I would play with you. There's lots of country boys that come to school. I'm a country girl. I mean, I live in town but really I'm a country girl."

Swiney looked at Rose for a long moment with eyes that seemed to be pleading, or hurt, she couldn't tell which. That look made Rose almost want to hug him.

"Come on," she said quickly. "Let's ask Abe."

They raced each other back to the house and burst in gasping and laughing.

"Lookit my floor!" Effie wailed. "You young-'uns get right back out on that porch and clean your shoes."

Rose and Swiney giggled as they scraped off their soles. Then they sobered themselves up and came in again. They waited patiently while Abe finished telling a story.

"What is it, Rose?" Mama asked, jiggling Elza in her lap. The baby reached with her tiny hands to grab Mama's nose.

Rose looked at Swiney, but he only bit his lip and looked back at her with scared eyes.

"Go on," she said. "Go on and ask."

"Well, I was just thinkin'," Swiney muttered. Then he blushed hard and clamped his mouth shut.

Rose huffed impatiently. "Swiney wants to know if he has a real name," she announced. "The town boys make fun of his name, and he thought maybe he had a proper one."

Abe laughed and put down his coffee cup. "Now Swiney-boy, why ain't you said nothing? Them city dudes been a-beating on you? Well, now, if that'd be the worriest thing on your head, I'm mighty proud to tell it. You got the same name as our great-grandpa: Nathan."

Swiney's mouth dropped open, and his eyes flew wide. "Nathan!" he shouted. "What kinda name is that?"

"It's a beautiful name," said Mama. "It's short for Nathaniel. A great writer had that name, Nathaniel Hawthorne. And a patriot of the Revolutionary War was Nathan Hale. Nowadays folks shorten it, to Nate."

"Nate," Swiney repeated slowly, as if tasting a new kind of food on his tongue.

"It's a good strong name," said Papa. "I guess there's no boy alive would make fun of a fellow named Nate."

"Nate," Swiney said again. Just then James cried out from Effie's lap, "'Ate!" Everyone burst out laughing, and James squealed with pleasure.

"Iffen it's good enough for baby James here, I reckon it's good enough for you . . . Nate," said Abe.

"Gosh, you mean I don't have to be Swiney no more?"

Rose wanted to correct his grammar, but she didn't dare spoil the shining, hopeful look on his face.

"I reckon it's your own name," Abe said. "You're a-getting to be a big growed-up boy. Iffen you got a idea to be Nate, I reckon you could be Nate."

"I'm Nate!" declared Nate, folding his arms across his chest, a fierce look of determination in his eyes. "You all got to call me Nate from now on."

But it wasn't so easy as that. Abe said he would always be Swiney-boy to him, but he promised always to try to call him Nate in front of strangers. Mama and Papa could remember, most of the time. For Rose it was more difficult. Swiney would always be Swiney to her, too.

She would always remember him to be the ragged, mussy boy Papa caught trying to steal Mama's eggs, whom they had gentled and whom Mama had taught to speak properly and have good manners. But Rose promised to try.

The next morning Rose hurriedly dressed for the first day of school. She was freed now from the chore of taking Bunting to pasture. She had liked doing it. It was pleasant to go for a walk out to the edge of town and hear the sounds of farmers at work in their fields, and spy a rabbit bounding away into a brush pile. But the pasture was grazed over and frost-killed. The cow would stay in the barn lot until the grass greened up again in the spring.

For the first time in her life, Rose could put on a crisp new dress—Mama had sewn one up from green-and-yellow-checked gingham—and look at all of herself in the mirror. The only mirror they owned on the farm was a little square one that hung on the wall by the front door, where Papa always shaved himself.

Now they had the long mirror on the door of the chifforobe. While Mama was out feeding and watering the chickens, Rose wriggled into the starchy dress, tied the white sash that Mama had made to go with it, pulled on her stockings and freshly greased brogans, and opened the chifforobe door.

First she looked at the dress. The fabric made her think of summer and flowers. The sash was very clever. It pulled the dress tight around her waist so that the skirt flared out around her legs. Rose liked the graceful shape it made, like a shock of wheat. She twisted this way and that, to see the fabric swirl like the fringe on the new parlor furniture.

Then she looked at her brown hair, pulled tightly over her head, and plaited into a single wide braid that reached far down her back. She wondered what she might look like with curled hair like Blanche's. Rose had never seen her back before, and she craned her neck a long time, seeing the new yellow ribbon that Mama had tied to her braid.

Then she looked at her face, the cheeks still shiny and pink from scrubbing. They were full cheeks, a little babyish, she thought. Her lips were bright red, as if she had just eaten a berry. Her gray eyes looked back at her gravely, the way a man looks at a horse he might like to buy.

All the time her stomach fluttered, and she tingled all over with excitement. The first day of school always wound her up. There were the smells of floors freshly oiled with floor-sweep, new chalk, and all those dinner pails that reminded her of a picnic. Almost all the girls would be wearing their newest dresses, and Rose would again have for her teacher Mrs. Honeycutt, whom she loved dearly.

Finally she was ready to leave. Rose didn't

need a dinner pail anymore, and she wouldn't ride to school on her donkey, like the girls who lived on farms. The new house sat just a hop, skip, and jump down the hill from school.

Mama helped her pull on her heavy winter coat. Rose put on her mittens, gathered up her slate and her Reader, and took one last look in the mirror of the hall tree to see that her tam-o'-shanter sat on her head at just the right tilt.

"Be a good girl and mind yourself walking to school," said Mama. "The ground is very slippery this morning."

It had rained the night before, and the cold earth froze the water into slick ice. All the trees and houses and fences sparkled. Rose nearly squealed with pleasure when she went outside and saw children all along the road, creeping up the hill and shrieking as they slipped and slid.

Blanche and Lois were in front of the Newtons', almost across the street from Rose's house, giggling helplessly. Blanche was trying to help Lois off the ground.

Rose minced her way down the walk.

"Oh, Rose. Come quick," Blanche cried out.

"Lois has new shoes, and the soles are so smooth she can hardly stand."

Rose and Blanche helped Lois to her feet, laughing themselves senseless.

"Oh, my poor bottom," Lois moaned, her face bright red from giggling. "I may never be able to sit on it again."

Rose was in heaven. For the first time since she had moved to the Ozarks, going to school was marvelous fun, and she was part of something outside herself. For the first time she wasn't afraid to walk into the schoolhouse on the first day and face a roomful of other children.

As they all clomped noisily up the stairs to the Fourth Reader, Rose looked about for Paul. Then she spied him through the door of the Sixth Reader, in a crowd of boys, telling a story. The way he brushed his hair from his forehead made her heart melt.

Finally all the Fourth Reader scholars had hung up their coats and hats and settled in their seats. Blanche and Lois sat together, but Rose didn't mind a bit. She sat right behind them, with Dora Hibbard. Dora and her twin sister, Cora, decided they didn't like to sit together anymore, but they still liked to play tricks on Mrs. Honeycutt. When she took the roll, Dora answered to Cora's name, and Cora answered to Dora's.

After Mrs. Honeycutt handed out peppermint sticks to all the scholars, they took up books. Jesse Gaskill was reciting from the Reader when suddenly the door flew open. Every head whirled to look, and there was Swiney's—Nate's—bright-red face, his scarf trailing behind like a long tail. A nervous titter ran through the room.

"Well, whom have we here? A new scholar?" Mrs. Honeycutt said. "And what might your name be?"

One of the boys snorted loudly, like a hog.

Swiney's eyes blazed angrily. "I'm Nate," he said loudly. "Nate Baird. That's my proper, rightful name. And any boy that wants to tell it different'll have me waitin' for him outside."

Now all the boys laughed wickedly. Nate took a step toward the boys' side of the room, dropped his dinner pail with a clatter, and raised his clenched fists. His tight jaw worked and pulsed.

"Silence!" Mrs. Honeycutt cried out, stalking down the aisle between the boys' seats. "That will be enough, or every one of you will stay in for recess.

"Now, Nate, I'll have no fighting in school. And I'm sure you know that you are expected to be here on time, when the bell rings."

"Yes'm," Nate said, looking nervously around the room. "I started out plenty early enough, but it was slippery as anything. Every time I took me a step ahead, I fell two steps back."

There was a hush of astonishment.

"But if that is true," Mrs. Honeycutt said, "however could you get here at all?"

"That was easy, ma'am," said Nate. "I just turned myself around and came backward."

The whole room exploded in laughter, and Nate's wide face broke out in a big sheepish grin. Mrs. Honeycutt showed him the cloak-room, where he hung his coat and put his dinner pail on the shelf.

When he came back out, two of the boys who had no seatmate called out, "Nate! Hey, Nate! Sit over here." Some of the boys even clapped him on the back as he took a seat with Jesse Gaskill.

Rose beamed with pride. Swiney—Nate—finally had come to school, and he had won his place by his wits instead of his fists. He was going to do just fine, and so was Rose. She just knew it would be a wonderful session, and she would love school as she never had before.

A Big Job

Nate didn't have a slate of his own, so while the other students quietly practiced their writing, he sat next to Mrs. Honeycutt at her desk, reciting very softly from a book of poems, and showing her his writing on a borrowed slate.

Rose could not keep her mind on her work. It was boring anyway, and she just had to watch Nate, his forehead furrowed in concentration, glancing at Mrs. Honeycutt now and then with a hopeful look in his eyes. Rose prayed with all her heart that he remembered the lessons Mama had taught him when they lived on the farm.

At recess Nate played one-eyed cat with the boys and showed them the peashooter he'd made from a hollowed-out stem of elderberry. Rose would have played, too, but some of those boys were rough, and she wouldn't take a chance of soiling her new dress for anything.

So she stayed with Blanche and Lois and the Hibbard twins. Blanche shared pieces of gum her father had given her from the drugstore. Rose watched Paul walk to the hitching shed with some other older boys, to look at the horses and mules.

"That's Paul Cooley, isn't it?" said Lois, playing with a curl of her yellow hair. "Didn't he come here with your family?"

"Yes," Rose said proudly. "He's going to be a telegrapher when he finishes school."

"I think he's awfully handsome," Lois said dreamily. "When I'm old enough, I wouldn't mind it a bit if he asked to walk me home from church."

Blanche, Dora, and Cora giggled, but there was no mirth in Rose's throat. A chill raced down her spine, and her heart seemed to stop in her breast.

She stared at Lois' bright face, her laughing eyes, her clear creamy skin, and then her caped mohair coat and her ribboned hat. Something wild and stormy blew up inside her. She had to turn away, as if her eyes had seen something too terrible to behold.

She stood digging her toes inside her shoes, helpless, tongue-tied, staring off at the hitching shed where Paul was running his hand down the neck of a horse.

Paul would *never* walk Lois home from church, she told herself fiercely. Why would he want to? Rose ought to know. She and Paul had been friends almost forever. Paul had never walked any girl home from church. Lois was just talking foolishness.

Rose shook herself against the chill air and uttered a long silent sigh of relief. It was impossible to think of Paul walking with anyone but Rose. It made so little sense that she could put it out of her mind, like a bad dream that melts away upon waking.

Rose made herself laugh at something Dora said, and by the time the bell rang, she was nearly herself again. The rest of the morning session she was so busy with her work, she had put any thoughts of Paul out of her mind.

When dinnertime came, Mrs. Honeycutt dismissed the scholars, but then she said, "Nate, would you come here, please?"

Rose got her coat and waited patiently, just near enough to hear.

"For a boy who has never been to school, you are a very good reader," she said. "But I think it would be best if you start in Professor Kay's Third Reader. There you will have a chance to improve your ciphering, grammar, and penmanship."

Rose's heart sank. Nate simply *must* stay in her class.

"But ma'am," Nate began to whine. "Can't I stay in the Fourth Reader? I like it here. I want to stay where Rose is. Oh, please don't send me downstairs. I'll try real hard. Honest, I will."

"Now, now. You will come back up, in time,"

said Mrs. Honeycutt, putting a hand on his shoulder. "I'm sure it will be only for this session. Professor Kay is a very good teacher, and I just know you will improve yourself quickly."

"Awww," Nate complained. His mouth wobbled and he looked at Rose pitifully.

Rose's mind whirled. There must be a way. Then, suddenly, she had an idea. "Mrs. Honeycutt?"

"Yes, Rose. What is it?"

"Mrs. Honeycutt, Nate is family to my family. He's got no mama and papa and he's 'most nearly a brother. Now that he's come to school, he's going to go with me to my house for dinner every day.

"Could we, may we, give Nate extra lessons? My mama was a teacher once, and we have given him all his lessons before this. I promise we will help him catch up to the others. Please, can he stay in the Fourth Reader?"

Mrs. Honeycutt smiled at Rose for a long moment, then looked at Nate. "It is a novel idea," she said slowly. "But I don't like to have a scholar who is too far behind the others."

"I promise we will study together, every day we can," Rose pressed on. Then she looked hard at Nate. "You will, won't you?"

"Sure, Rose. If you say it. But I got to get on home after school. I've my chores to do."

Mrs. Honeycutt slipped the cap onto her pen with a click and gathered up her books. "In any case, I cannot make such a decision on my own. You are a good student, Rose, and I know your mother is quite devoted to books and learning. But I must discuss it with Professor Kay."

All during dinner, Nate and Rose talked and talked, trying to divine what Professor Kay might say.

"I'm not coming to school if I can't stay in your same class," said Nate, stuffing a piece of corn bread in his mouth. "I'm too growed-up to be with babies."

"*Grown*-up. And don't speak with your mouth full," Mama scolded. "A quitter never wins, and a winner never quits, Swi—I mean Nate. I'm sure Professor Kay and Mrs. Honeycutt will decide the question for the best of everyone.

"You are a smart boy, and a quick learner. A

few months in the Third Reader won't hurt you any. But if you stay in the Fourth, we will do what we can to help you catch up.

"You can study with Rose, and I will do what I am able. There's Sunday, too, although heaven knows where I'll find time. Between church and the Eastern Star, and all the social obligations of living in town, it's a wonder I have a moment to take a breath."

Nate helped Rose wash and dry the dishes so they could hurry back to school before the bell. They spotted Mrs. Honeycutt in Professor Kay's classroom, and stood by the doorway waiting for her. Nate pulled at his lip, shifted from foot to foot, and sighed loudly.

"Be still!" Rose hissed. "You're making me all jittery."

Professor Kay stood up to stretch and saw them. "Hello there, children. Why don't you step on in here?"

Soberly they walked into Professor Kay's room. Professor Kay smiled through his long, tobacco-stained beard, leaned against his desk, and motioned for them to sit down. Mrs. Honeycutt stood with her hands clasped in front of her.

"Mrs. Honeycutt has been telling me of your dilemma," he said. "It's Nate, is it? Well, then, Nate. I take it you are a hill boy. Where do your folks come from?"

"Arkansas," said Nate. His leg was jiggling.

"Are you a trapper?"

"Yes sir," said Nate. "I got . . . I mean, I have my own trap lines."

Professor Kay tugged thoughtfully on his beard.

"And what do you trap?"

"Skunks, rabbits, mostly. Once I caught me a fox. Mr. Nelson gave six bits for it."

"He did? And what does he give for skunks?"

"Fifteen cents for a regular old polecat, twenty-five cents if it's got only a smidge of white or if it's purely black."

"I see," said Professor Kay, walking to the blackboard and picking up a piece of chalk. "Let's say you had yourself six regular skunk pelts, and one that was all black. How much would Nelson give you then?" He wrote on the blackboard, "6 x 15¢," and "1 x 25¢."

Nate stared blankly at those numbers for a moment. Then he said, "I wouldn't take a nickel off him."

Professor Kay's eyes lit up. "You wouldn't. Now why is that?"

"'Cause he cheats. Mr. Reynolds gives a whole dollar for a fox. And my brother says Nelson puts navy beans to stretch his coffee, and he flours up his lard."

Mrs. Honeycutt tittered and blushed, and Professor Kay barked out a laugh.

"I guess you've learned one valuable lesson," he said. "Once burned, twice shy. But let's say you sold your pelts at these prices." Professor Kay tapped on the board with his chalk. "What would you get?"

Nate's forehead bunched in thought. His lips moved, and he buried his face in his hands for a moment, making a little humming noise under his breath.

Rose crossed her fingers. Please, Nate, please, she prayed.

Nate agonized for the longest time. Then, finally, he looked up at Professor Kay and his shoulders sagged. "I can't figure it, sir."

Rose's heart sank, but Professor Kay only chuckled.

"Well, son, I reckon what you lack in learning you might make up for in pluck. But you've got a big job before you. Mrs. Honeycutt tells me chickens have better penmanship, and your grammar isn't up to snuff. But if you children are willing to work hard together, I guess a try is better than nothing."

"Thank you, so much!" Rose burbled. "Thank you, Professor Kay. Thank you, Mrs. Honeycutt."

"Yahoo!" Nate cried out. He jumped up from his seat and grabbed Rose in a crushing hug.

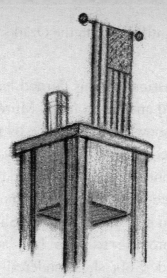

The Debate

"*Pro*-crastination," Rose said. "Not Percrastination. You keep writing it wrong." She scrubbed her slate clean with a damp rag. "Do it again."

Nate huffed irritably. "What's it mean, anyway?" From far away came the shrieks and laughter of children playing.

"Putting off doing a thing. Just write it down: *Procrastination is the thief of time.*"

Nate took another sugar cookie from the plate and grinned at her while he took a bite. "Who cares about a dumb old word like that? I never heard a person say it, not once. I'd just as leave percrastination this darned lesson. Let's get your sled and go on up to Murray's Hill. I reckon the snow's as slick as ice by now."

Rose glared at Nate in silent fury. He was so feisty and contrary, she just wanted to slap him. She could see he was pretending not to understand, just to get under her skin. She meant to keep her promise to help him stay in the Fourth Reader, but she wondered sometimes why she bothered.

It was hard work teaching him his lessons, harder than Rose had ever imagined. With teaching Nate piled on top of her chores and her own schoolwork, and her reading, by bedtime she was too tired even to brush her hair.

Rose got up from the kitchen table and marched into Mama and Papa's bedroom. She fetched one of Mama's pads of paper from the chifforobe, slammed the drawer shut, and brought the pad back into the kitchen, slapping it down in front of Nate. She stood over him with her hands on her hips.

"Write it down, twenty times!" she barked. "With every 't' and 'h' exactly twice as tall as a vowel and every 'f' exactly three times as tall, and every 't' crossed, and every 'i' dotted. And not with little circles, either. You better do as I say, or I'll tell Mama."

"All right, all right," he muttered. They both knew Mama would never stand for Nate's fussing and fuming.

He took the pencil and began to write, very slowly, with his thumb clumsily folded over his index finger.

"You aren't even holding your pencil properly," Rose complained. "I showed you, like this. How can you ever expect your letters to be right if you hold it like that?"

"Dunno," Nate muttered. "I can't do it like that, see?" He scribbled some nonsense, and then went back to his work, his thumb over his index finger again.

Rose couldn't bear to watch, so she busied herself putting up a pot of beans to simmer on the stove. Fido lay stretched out on the floor, his paws twitching with dreams.

It was Saturday. Mama and Papa came home from trading at Reynolds', bringing in a gust of cold air and stamping their boots. The first snow had fallen the night before, and a bright, bitter cold day had followed the storm. While Rose put away the flour and salt, Mama looked over Nate's shoulder.

"It's an improvement," she said, pulling off her gloves. "But your 'f's are still too short, and you must try to space your letters so your sentences won't scrunch up at the end."

"Yes'm," Nate said politely, which only made Rose mad again because he wouldn't listen to her the way he listened to Mama.

At dinner Mama said they would all take their baths early, after they ate. "There's to be a debate tonight, at the Opera House, and I don't want to lose a good seat waiting for the water to heat."

"What's a debate?" Nate wanted to know.

"It is an entertainment," said Mama. "Folks gather together and discuss a question. I've never been, but I think it must be very interesting. Now finish up so we can get the dishes washed and start the bathwater warming."

After dinner Abe came by to fetch Nate to

help deliver a load of stove wood in town.

"You ought to come tonight," Mama told Abe. "There will be refreshments after, and it might be a chance for Effie to come out after being cooped up so long with the babies."

"Now I like to see a good scrap," he said. "Just maybe I'll study on it."

They ate a hurried supper of leftover sweet potatoes and venison stew that Mama cooked with meat from a deer Abe had shot. Then they quickly changed into their good clothes over their warm union suits. Soon they were bundled up and walking uptown under a glittering ceiling of stars that seemed to hang just above the rooftops.

The frozen crust of the snow had been trampled everywhere, and it squeaked under their shoes. They had to walk carefully, holding on to each other, to keep from slipping and tripping on the icy ruts. The snow in the street had been stirred up and soiled by the heavy Saturday traffic of horses and wagons.

Lamps glittered in the windows of the houses. Here and there small clutches of people were also making their way to the Opera House, and a few wagons passed them.

They caught up to Mrs. Rippee, and Papa let go of Mama's arm to help her over the humps of ice.

"Gracious me," chuckled Mrs. Rippee. "Wouldn't you know there'd be a snowstorm when Mr. Rippee is away on business and couldn't get home? Thank you, Mr. Wilder. You're very kind, I'm sure."

"I haven't heard yet," said Mama. "What is the topic for discussion?"

"Oh, a very good topic, one that is guaranteed to stir the folks up. Resolved: Who has been more cruelly treated, the Negro or the Indian. What is your opinion?"

"I don't know," said Mama. "The question never came to my mind, but I think it is a hard one to answer."

"Oops!" Mrs. Rippee whooped as she stumbled, and Papa caught her. She giggled girlishly. "That is the feature of a debate that makes it most interesting. The question is always unanswerable. The debaters must use all their powers of persuasion to win. Last winter we debated which was the most destructive force, fire or water."

"Now there's a tough one," said Papa.

Rose knew right away what she thought. "Fire!" she blurted. Their home on the prairie had been destroyed by a fire Rose had accidentally started when she was a very small. A stove fire had nearly burned their house on Rocky Ridge Farm, and just that summer a great fire had burned over some of their fields and almost destroyed the orchard. Rose was terrified of fire.

"Rose, mind your manners!" Mama chided.

"Oh, I don't mind a bit," said Mrs. Rippee. "In fact, Rose, most folks said it was fire. But the team that debated on the side of water won the prize. Water could put out fire, but fire could not put out water. Well, here we are."

A crowd of people swarmed around the door next to the Boston Racket Store. They followed it inside, up a long flight of steep stairs, to a big open room lit with kerosene lamps all along the walls. At one end was a raised platform, with curtains drawn back on either side. The room was hazy with coal-oil smoke and full of lively chatter and the sounds of chairs being moved.

Rose spied many faces she knew. It seemed everyone in town had come. She saw Blanche's mother, but she didn't see Blanche. Mr. Reynolds, who owned the store where Mama traded, stood on the platform. And there was Paul.

"Hey, Rose." He smiled. "What're you doing here?"

"I guess I can come to a debate if I want to," she said saucily.

Paul was dressed in a crisp dark suit, with a starched collar. Rose was startled to see that he was wearing a pocket watch chain, draped across his vest, just the way Papa did when he dressed up.

"It was my papa's," Paul explained. He pulled out the silver-cased watch, clicked it open, and showed it to Rose. The back of it had a raised picture of a locomotive, with smoke trailing from its stack, and telegraph wires. It was beautiful, heavy and solid, the way she remembered Mr. Cooley.

"It's very handsome," said Rose, not knowing just what to say.

Just then Mr. Reynolds called out, "Folks! Folks! If you will find yourselves seats, we can get on with our debate tonight."

"Come sit with us!" Rose said quickly, looking to see where Mama and Papa had gone.

"I've already got my seat, with the Beaumonts. They asked me to sit with them. Gosh, imagine that, Rose. He's the president of the bank. See you later." And then he vanished, swallowed up by the throng.

The Beaumonts, Rose grumbled to herself as she pushed through the crowd looking for Mama and Papa. I just bet that old Lois had something to do with it. She looked around, to see if Lois was there, but she was too short to peer over the shoulders of all those grown-ups. Then she found Mrs. Rippee, and they went to sit with Mama and Papa.

Rose only half heard Mr. Reynolds as he explained the debate. She kept turning around to see where Paul was sitting. "Be still!" Mama whispered.

"Two teams will be chosen," Mr. Reynolds said. "The captain of the team for the Negro will be James Loftin, and for the Indian it will be Cyrus Waters."

Mr. Loftin and Mr. Waters stepped up onto the stage. Then they began to pick two other people for each of their teams. Rose gasped when Mr. Waters said, "I'll have Almanzo Wilder. He's the smartest horse trader I know."

Everyone laughed. Rose gasped. Papa's head jerked. He turned and stared at Mama with such a look of puzzlement that Rose burst out giggling. Papa was never befuddled by anything.

He glanced around himself shyly, and then slowly stood up. He coughed once, and said in a loud, clear voice, "I thank you for the honor, Waters. But it will be better for you if you ask somebody else. You folks all know a good horse trader lets the horse speak for itself."

Everyone laughed again. Mama tried to hide her smile behind her hand, but her face had turned bright red. Rose was rocking with excitement. To see Papa holding the attention of all those people, all those smiling faces turned to listen to him, was spine-tingling.

"Well, all right then," Mr. Waters said. "Let me take a look at my list of names."

Papa began to sit down, but suddenly he sprang to his feet again and called out, "If you like, I can suggest a name."

"Sure enough," Mr. Waters said.

"I reckon a fine orator on the subject would be a body who's at least known some Indians."

Papa shot a sidelong glance at Mama, who stared back in frozen horror. Rose could not believe her ears.

"Now, Mrs. Wilder grew up in Indian Territory, and there's no subject she doesn't hold a strong opinion on."

"Manly Wilder!" Mama growled.

A nervous ripple of creaking seats and uncertain muttering ran through the room. Rose hunched down in her chair, to get out of the way of all those eyes that were looking toward

Mama and Papa. She felt a wave of hot blood wash up her neck and into her cheeks.

"There aren't any rules on it," Mr. Reynolds said, "but, well, we never had a lady in a debate before."

Papa grinned and looked around the room. "I don't have to tell any of you fellows, when it comes to arguing there's not a woman alive couldn't hold her own."

The room filled with hearty laughter.

"And I'm here to say you won't catch Mrs. Wilder without a last word or two. You will have to hurry to get ahead of her in any debate. I've been tryin' for twelve years and I ain't won one yet!"

That brought the biggest laugh. The whole room throbbed with it. A man sitting behind Papa pounded him on the shoulder.

Now Mama was tugging at Papa's jacket to get him to sit down. "No, no!" she cried. "I couldn't. Not in front of all these people. Land sakes, Manly, *do sit down*!"

But Papa wouldn't sit. He leaned over and whispered, "It's all in good fun, Bess. Be a good sport about it."

Instantly Mama pulled herself together, sat up straight, and clutched her hands in her lap. She looked around at the staring people, blinking rapidly and nodding with a tight, desperate smile.

"Well, Waters, what do you have to say to that?" Mr. Reynolds asked when the racket had died away.

"I reckon Wilder wins his point. Mrs. Wilder, will you favor us with your expert knowledge?"

Papa grabbed Mama gently by the arm and helped her out of her chair. Mama's hand flew to her hair. Then she smoothed her dress, took a deep breath, and walked to the stage. Mama stood stock-still next to Mr. Waters while the two men picked their last teammates.

Rose thought she looked just beautiful up there in her black cashmere dress. Mama had had that same dress for as long as Rose could remember, but every so often she would make a stylish new collar for it. Just that week Mama had finished sewing up a three-cornered sailor collar with a wide embroidered flare that covered her bosom and almost all of her shoulders.

Mama's rosy face looked like the center of a morning glory in full bloom.

Then the two teams left the room, to choose who would speak for them. Two girls from the Sixth Reader at school came onto the platform and recited poetry, but Rose heard none of it. Her mind was racing. She was so proud of Mama, and shocked that Papa had put her up to it. She craned her neck to see where Paul was sitting, and if Blanche was there.

Finally the teams came back and filed onto the platform. The debate began. Mr. Loftin's team went first.

"I will speak for the Negro," Mr. Loftin said. "We all know about the sorrow of slavery, and the tragedy it brought upon our country. But what do we know of the black man's suffering, of how he was torn from his homeland by force, made to cross the treacherous ocean in irons, often separated from his family, and then bought and sold like livestock?"

He went on and on, and Rose sat on the edge of her seat, eating up every word. For the first time, Rose learned of the terrible history of the

Negroes, of how they were treated as beasts of burden, made to do the most hateful work for nothing more than the barest food to eat.

"The white man will bear the shame of slavery until the end of time," Mr. Loftin said. Rose remembered the colored-only waiting room at the depot. It was small and had no door, but the whites-only waiting room was big, and had a heating stove, and a door.

She wondered how it could be that Mr. Loftin could argue for the cruelty of the white man against the Negro and yet not work to end the Negro's suffering.

Finally he said, "And therefore, I believe it is beyond arguing that the Negro has been treated more cruelly than the Indian."

The audience applauded long and loud, and then it was the turn of Mr. Waters' team.

"Being as how we men have had no experience with Indians, and Mrs. Wilder has been a teacher to boot, we have decided to let her speak for us," he said.

"That's my Bess," Papa called out proudly.

Mama stepped to the center of the stage and

began to speak. Her eyes sparkled in the lamp-light, and Rose shivered with expectation. Mama looked so small and lonely up there, all by herself.

"It is a very difficult matter to measure cruelty," she said, her beautiful clear voice filling every corner of that big hall. "It is nearly an act of cruelty to try to do it, as if one race could be said to be more fortunate than another simply because it has suffered a bit less misery and sorrow.

"But I must speak for the Indian and it is with great conviction, for the Indian has had no voice raised on his behalf. Yes, slavery was cruel. Even today in many places the Negro still does not enjoy the freedoms of white folks.

"But in being enslaved, the Negro was provided for, given a roof over his head, clothing to wear, and food for his table. Once his terrible journey to America was over, he had no more wars to fight. To live, to raise his children, he learned to bow to his masters.

"The Indian was driven from his land. It was taken from him, at the point of a gun, to satisfy the greed of men whose only interest was gold, timber, and farmland.

"His game was killed, his forests cut down, and he was pushed farther and farther west, onto the territories of other tribes who naturally wanted to protect their homelands from invaders.

"Everywhere he looked, the Indian was surrounded by enemies. If he tried to stay and fight, the white man sent armies with weapons the Indians could not obtain. The arrow and the knife were no match for the Winchester and the Hotchkiss gun.

"The white man hunted the Indian down like a deer, and was sometimes not satisfied to kill just the braves, but slaughtered also the women and the children.

"The Indian leaders who chose to obey the white man's orders, and to believe the false promises, signed treaties they could not read. When they settled in the new lands, the white man cheated the Indian again, and forced him to emigrate still farther, onto lands that were foreign to him, lands that were worthless and arid, that did not give him the game he needed to make his clothing and feed his family.

"And all the while the white man was cheating the Indian, he said to himself, 'The only good Indian is a dead Indian.'

"Tribe fought with tribe, and then when their numbers were diminished and they joined together, they were weakened, and it was too late. The white man had settled the land, laid the railroads, and killed off the buffalo. There was nothing left but suffering, hunger, and disease. An ancient civilization was destroyed."

Tears welled up in Rose's eyes, and she noticed that two women sitting near her had their handkerchiefs in their hands. The room was very still. Somewhere someone coughed.

"Our forefathers wrote in the Declaration of Independence that all men are created equal. We know that they could not have believed it to be true, because even as those words were written, the Negro was living in slavery and the white man was stealing away the very lives of the Indians. We cannot forget that it was the Indians who, when the Pilgrims faced their first winter without food, fed them and taught them to grow corn.

"But the promise of personal freedom guaranteed by the Constitution was given only to those who already had it.

"Now, finally, the Negro has been granted his emancipation, and the right to own his land, and to travel and worship as he pleases, but the Indian is no better off than he has been since the white man came to this place. After all, it is just seven years since the terrible massacre of innocent, unarmed Sioux at Wounded Knee.

"Yes, some folks would say that the Indians did their share of stealing and killing as well. When I was a child living in Indian Territory, my family lived in fear that the Indians would rise up against us settlers. My father had built his house on Indian lands by mistake, right on an old Indian hunting trail.

"But I also remember that when the Indians met by a creek near our little house to form a council of war against the whites, it was an Osage chief who saved us. His name was Soldat du Chêne, and I might not be standing here today had he not pledged his warriors to protect us from the other tribes."

Heads nodded, and a murmur ran through the crowd. Rose glanced at Papa. His eyes shone fiercely.

"It is interesting for me to remember, as well, that when I lived in that little house, we once all came down deathly sick with ague. The only doctor who rode all those miles into the Indian wilderness to tend to us was Dr. Tan. And he was a Negro."

The audience gasped. So did Rose.

"So if I must weigh the question of who has suffered the greatest cruelty, I must argue that in a country where a Negro has the freedom and the possibility to become a doctor, but where Indians are still hunted down like animals, it is the Indian who has suffered the most."

Mama stopped speaking and looked at Mr. Reynolds with questioning eyes. For a long moment the room stayed strangely silent. Then the applause began, slowly at first, and then building until it crashed in great waves around the room. Mama blushed and stepped backward to stand by Mr. Waters, but he gently pushed her forward again.

Then people began to stand, and there was whistling and cheering. No one had to be told that Mama had won the debate.

Every nerve in Rose's body tingled. She had never known the things that Mama told that night. And she had never guessed that Mama could speak so powerfully, to make people see and feel things they had never seen before or felt.

Rose's heart overflowed with love and pride. When she could finally squeeze through the clutch of people surrounding Mama and congratulating her, she gave her a big tight hug.

Mr. Craig

After the debate there wasn't a soul in Mansfield who didn't know who Mama was, and about the wonderful talk she had given. The next day in church, the whole congregation applauded when Reverend Davis mentioned it in his sermon.

The next time Rose went with Mama to Reynolds', everyone on the streets and in the store greeted her.

"I ain't never laid eyes on nary Injun nor Negro," said a farmer they didn't know. "But you purely opened my eyes to some things, and I been studyin' on the question ever since."

Every day when Papa came home from his drayage, he told them of someone who had passed along a compliment. "Why, there's folks talking about it all the way to Hartville and Ava. You beat the nation at speechifying, Bess."

"I had no idea I even had it in me," said Mama. "I have never been so angry as when you put me up for it, Manly. And standing on that stage, I thought I might faint dead away with fright. But I suppose it came out all right in the end.

"You know the ladies of the Eastern Star want to collect donations to send to an Indian reservation to help buy books and school things. And they are voting me to be a Worthy Matron. I just feel so much a part of this little town now."

There was even a story about the debate in the weekly newspaper, the *Mansfield Mail*:

Our own Mrs. A. J. Wilder held an appreciative audience in thrall with her electrifying talk on the calamities that have befallen the

Negro and Indian races in this country. Mrs. Wilder herself grew up among Indians, and her telling of some of those experiences brought the good citizens of our town to their feet at the end.

With compliments to Mr. Loftin's team for the Negro, when the debate was ended it was a hands-down opinion by all in attendance that the poor Indians had finally won a fight.

Papa brought home extra copies of the paper. They cut out the story and sent one to Grandma and Grandpa Ingalls in South Dakota, and another to Papa's family in Louisiana.

After some days things settled down. On Rose's eleventh birthday Mama made a chicken pie and a gingerbread cake with sugar icing. She and Papa gave Rose her first very own hairbrush. It had sturdy Russian bristles and a smooth aluminum handle that would never tarnish, and there was an aluminum comb to go with it.

Rose decided to keep them in Mama and Papa's room, in a drawer in the chifforobe.

That way, when she came down the ladder in the morning, it would be handy for her to brush her long hair looking in the big mirror.

The week before Christmas things livened up again. Rose and Mama helped decorate the church Christmas tree. Papa gave Rose a little pile of nickels to buy presents; that was the most fun of all.

Mama took her to Reynolds', where she bought little sacks of candy for the Baird babies, a pink hair ribbon for Effie, a celluloid comb for Nate's unruly hair, and a china mug for Abe. It had a clever little shelf inside the lip with a hole in it to keep his mustache from getting wet when he drank his coffee.

When she was done, she had one nickel left. She was going to give it back to Papa, but she decided at the last minute to buy a bow tie for Paul in a beautiful red-and-blue-plaid silk. It cost six cents, so she added a penny of her own.

She had knitted a new fascinator for Mama, and embroidered a handkerchief for Papa, to go with his good suit.

Abe brought them their Christmas turkey.

"It's a big one, too," Mama crooned. "We'll have to have company for dinner. Maybe the Cooleys will come."

"Yes, ma'am," said Abe. "I got me five big turkeys, with one shot."

"How could you do that?" Rose wondered suspiciously. "It's just one of your stories, isn't it?"

"Little girl, this ain't no story," Abe said earnestly. "You go and ask Effie or Swiney-boy—Nate—your own self. I was out a-walking through that corn patch, the one we ain't never cut on account of the dry weather killed it.

"I seen this here flock of turkeys and passed around in front of 'em whilst they was a-walking in line, one behind the other, between two rows.

"The first old tom laid his eye on me and stopped, and the others closed up tight so they was all a-standing in a line. I aimed my gun at the neck of the first one, and when the smoke blew off, I had me five full-grown birds. It was a mighty heavy load to carry."

That was such a rich-feeling Christmas, so

different from the quiet, simple Christmases of the past three years on Rocky Ridge Farm. There were visits with the neighbors, and to the Cooleys and to Blanche's house.

The Cooleys stopped by on Christmas Eve, for cake and cider in the parlor. Mama and Mrs. Cooley were in the kitchen, and George had gone out to the barn with Papa to give Bunting her Christmas corn.

Paul sat on the tête-à-tête in the parlor, flipping through a copy of *Youth's Companion*, which was a magazine that Papa sometimes brought home. Rose dashed up to her room and brought back the bow tie. A jolt of excitement ran through her as she handed it to him, wrapped in store paper and tied with a bit of string. She plopped down beside him, sat on her hands, and hugged her elbows to her side.

Paul looked at her in wonderment. "Gosh," he said, "a present for me?"

"Just open it, you old hen."

He untied the string and pulled back the paper. His eyes lit up.

"Shucks, it's first-rate, Rose. And it'll go swell

with my blue suit. But I don't have anything to give you back."

"I don't care," Rose said, and meant it. "It's just fun to give you a Christmas present. I never did that before."

And then Paul did a most shocking thing. He leaned forward and brushed a light kiss on her cheek. Rose was so surprised she jumped back, and then blushed hard.

"I'm . . . I'm sorry," she stammered. "It's just . . . well . . . you startled me."

Paul grinned shyly. "Golly, Rose. You sure are sweet. Seems like we've been friends since time began. If ever I had a sister, I'd want her to be just like you."

Rose's knees melted from under her. She felt a quick beat of remorse, but then shook it off. That was the nicest thing Paul had ever said to her, and she basked in the glow of his gentle smile.

That was a moment that Rose wished would never end. The cozy house seemed to be holding her in a gentle, warm embrace. The murmur of voices in the kitchen, the clopping of horses' hooves outside, and the crunch of wood settling in the heater stove sounded to her like notes in a melody.

There were curtains on all the windows, and furniture in all the rooms. Decorated with branches of cedar and bittersweet, full of the good smells of baking cakes and pies and cookies, the house finally felt like home. And town felt like home, too.

On Christmas morning Rose's stocking bulged with candy, nuts, two oranges, and even a bar of toilet soap, scented with lavender. Rose had never seen toilet soap. All her life she had used the slimy soft soap that was cooked from the fat of a hog and lye water.

The perfumed soap smelled so good, it would be a shame to use it up. So she tucked it in a drawer of her little chest upstairs, where its scent crept into her union suits and stockings and made them smell like spring every time she put on a fresh pair.

Papa gave Rose a pictorial history of the Civil War, and Mama gave her a beautiful golden brooch in the shape of a clover leaf, with a red garnet in the middle that sparkled when she held it in the lamplight. She couldn't wait to wear it to school.

One day, right after New Year's, Papa brought a visitor home to supper. Mama and Rose cooked up a company meal in the kitchen while Papa sat in the parlor talking with Mr. Craig. Fido scratched at the back door, but Mama wouldn't let him in when they had a guest in to eat.

Mama sent Rose to change into her best dress, wound her long braid up in a bun, and fussed over the food the way she did when the Eastern Star ladies came visiting.

"Who is he?" Rose wanted to know.

Mama shushed Rose and closed the kitchen door. "He used to be a schoolteacher and principal," she whispered. "He's just finished his law studies and is going to work at the bank. We want to make a good impression. He might be interested in boarding here."

"Boarding? You mean he might stay in our house?"

"That's what boarders do, Rose. He's very

refined, and well educated. Turn those pork chops. Smells like they might be getting ready to burn."

Rose reeled at the thought of a stranger living with them. She couldn't imagine it.

"But why?"

"Boarders pay for their meals and and a room to sleep. It's called bed and board. That's what we have the extra bedrooms for, to make a little extra cash money.

"It was only a matter of time 'til we had the furniture and found someone suitable. Papa's been looking for weeks now, but we thought it better to wait until after Christmas. I do hope he likes my cooking."

When they sat down to eat, Rose stared so hard at Mr. Craig that Mama had to kick her under the table.

"You have a very comfortable home," he said, smiling at Mama. "And the supper smells delicious."

Mr. Craig was tall and thin, and everything about him was clean and neat. He sat very straight and proper, and glanced about with owlish eyes that saw everything but told nothing.

His mustache was perfectly trimmed, and his brown hair was combed as tidily as if he had just stepped out of a barbershop. He was dressed as crisply as a freshly made bed, with a snowy white collar that had a gold stay pin at the throat, and cuffs with shiny gold links. His dark tie hung perfectly straight down the front, and he cut his pork chops with quick, precise movements.

Rose jumped when Mama kicked her again, harder this time. "Eat your supper, dear," she said, glaring at Rose.

"Yes, it is an up-and-coming town," Mr. Craig was saying to Papa. "With the new rail line going into Ava, there will be many opportunities. These turnips are buttered and seasoned to perfection, Mrs. Wilder. I don't know when was the last time I ate so well."

"Do have another helping, Mr. Craig," Mama said in her most polite voice. "I'm afraid we are eating quite a lot of turnips this winter. The drought took a terrible toll on the gardens and crops."

"Your father tells me you are in the Fourth Reader," Mr. Craig said, looking at Rose with his blank, piercing eyes. "How do you find the teachers in your school?"

"Mrs. Honeycutt is very nice," Rose said flatly. "But the lessons are boring."

"Rose!" Mama scolded. "Our daughter is very quick, perhaps too quick at times," she said, turning an embarrassed smile upon Mr. Craig. "She is quite an avid reader, and I'm afraid she is ahead of her schoolmates."

"Yes, it is a challenge for a teacher to guide each and every scholar at his own pace," said Mr. Craig. "But you will find your lessons very useful when you are grown up," he told Rose. "We learn not for school but for life."

Rose decided right then and there that she didn't like Mr. Craig. The conversation was stiff and achingly dull. And she couldn't speak when she wanted to. She prayed he wouldn't stay.

When dinner was over, and Rose was stuck in the kitchen washing the dishes, Mama, Papa, and Mr. Craig looked at the front bedroom that was next to the parlor.

" . . . quite suitable, I'm sure," she heard Mr. Craig say. Then they went into the parlor, and Mama shut the door.

Rose fumed and slam-banged the pots and pans as she worked. She hated the idea that any room in their house would belong to someone else. Sometimes she liked to go into that front bedroom and peer through the curtains at the traffic passing on the street. Or she would lie on the bed reading a book and munching an apple.

She knew better than to complain. They needed the extra cash money. But she didn't have to like it, and maybe Mr. Craig wouldn't stay long.

He moved in the very next evening, just before dinner. Then Rose found she had something extra to grumble about.

"We will wear our second-best dresses for meals from now on," said Mama. "And Papa will wear his good coat. Don't pout, Rose. I know it is a bother, but I won't have us coming to the table looking like tramps."

The whole rhythm of the house changed. Mama shut poor Fido outdoors, or in the kitchen on bitter cold days, so he could not lie at Rose's feet during meals. There was extra food to cook, extra dishes to wash, and the house to be kept spotless, now that they had company all the time. Mama pounced on every speck of dust until a fly would slip and break its neck. There was more laundry, too. Mr. Craig paid Mama to clean and press his shirts and collars.

They must be quiet in the morning before Mr. Craig got up, and after dinner when he went to his room. Worst of all, during meals she had to sit and listen to Mama and Papa talk about business and other grown-up affairs with Mr. Craig.

Rose so missed the conversations the family had had at that table. Mama and Papa liked Mr. Craig. They were glad to have him in the house, and always greeted him cheerfully. But Rose felt herself being pushed aside. She began more and more to keep her thoughts to herself.

Boarders to Feed

A few weeks after Mr. Craig moved in, Papa brought to supper two men who worked for the railroad. They were surveyors from Philadelphia, a big city back east. They had come to the Ozarks to map out the grades for the new railroad spur that would bring freight to Mansfield from Ava, about ten miles south.

Talk of the new spur was on everybody's lips. It would bring more business to Mansfield. There would be more traveling men to stay in the hotels and eat in the restaurants; more timber, crops, and livestock to ship; more settlers; and more business for everyone. A boom time was coming.

Papa had driven the men and their surveying equipment out to the countryside in his dray-wagon. They spent their days marking the route the rails would take.

Papa had told them what a good cook Mama was, and that they couldn't find a better or cheaper meal in town. So even though they slept in the hotel, they came to the Wilders for supper, and each man paid Mama forty cents for his board.

Now the dining table was full of men talking business. So Rose and Mama stayed in the kitchen, and Nate, too, during the week. They bustled about getting pots and bowls of food to the table, filling pitchers, pouring coffee and cutting pie, and taking away empty plates.

They ate their own suppers in hurried mouthfuls at the little table in the kitchen. At least Fido could sit at Rose's feet in there. The men's deep muffled voices seeped through the closed door from the dining room.

"That's some wild country down there," one

of the surveyors said. "There are farmers living out in those hills who have never seen a steam engine. Imagine that, it's darn near the dawn of the twentieth century with all its gadgets and contraptions—the telephone, the moving picture, the automobile—and those folks are living just the same as their grandfathers."

Rose, Mama, and Nate all leaned toward the door to the hear better.

"Down near Ava we camped out some nights, and the country is so rough, a man has to sleep with his pistol under his bedroll."

"That's right," said the other one. "Old Will there shot a wolf right in our camp of a night. He was standing there bold as brass helping himself to our bacon."

Soon the surveyors came to eat every evening, and for Sunday dinner as well. When their work was done and they left town, they bragged about Mama's cooking to other railroad men who were coming to Mansfield to hire the grading crews and set up the supply shop. Those men came to eat at Mama's table, too.

Rose was working harder and harder now.

There was no time anymore to teach Nate his lessons at dinner each day, but Mrs. Honeycutt said he was doing well enough to keep up on his own.

One day Rose took Nate with her to visit Mrs. Rippee, who lent him a book about a poor boy who saved a train from wrecking and made his fortune digging for gold. The title was *Digging for Gold: A Story of California*, and the man who wrote that book was Horatio Alger, Jr. Mrs. Rippee said Mr. Alger was famous and wealthy from writing books about such boys.

Nate's eyes shone with excitement as she handed it to him. "It is a story of rags to riches," Mrs. Rippee said. "I think you will find it quite inspirational."

Nate quickly scanned the first page. "What's a skinflint?" he asked.

Mrs. Rippee chuckled. "A nickel-nurser," she said. "Someone who is miserly with money. See now? You have learned a new word already."

All the next weeks the only thing Nate

wanted to do was read that book. He stayed inside at recess reading it. He sneaked reading it during lessons, until Mrs. Honeycutt caught him and made him put it away. He laid it next to his plate at dinner in the kitchen, until Mama had to scold him to eat.

Every minute he was asking Rose the meaning of another word, or how to say it. And he pestered her to listen while he read the exciting parts.

Even Abe complained one day when he brought a load of firewood.

"That boy's gone plain work-lazy," he told Mama. "He's all the time a-reading that durn book."

"It is a stage," Mama consoled him. "When a child discovers the world of books and stories, it is all he ever wants at first. Rose was just the same. Let him read, as much as you can."

One Sunday afternoon Rose and Nate lay sprawled across the bed in the extra bedroom, reading.

Mama and Papa were out visiting with the

Helfinstines. Rose was so deeply buried in her book she didn't notice that Mr. Craig was standing in the doorway, until she heard the rattle of the newspaper he had been reading in the parlor.

Rose jumped up. "I didn't see you. Is there something you wanted?"

"Nothing at all," Mr. Craig said. "I was just thinking what a great comfort it is to see young folks so absorbed in their books. May I see what you have been reading?"

Rose and Nate handed him their books. "*Digging for Gold*," Mr. Craig read out. "How do you find this story?"

"Gosh, it's the best," Nate said. "When I grow up some, I'm going to do just like Grant Colburn. I'm going to make my fortune and take care of my people."

"And you are reading *Treasure Island*, by Robert Louis Stevenson," Mr. Craig said to Rose. "Also a stirring tale."

"Yes sir," Rose said politely. But she didn't like to be interrupted in the middle of reading.

Mr. Craig thumbed through *Treasure Island*

for a few moments. In the awkward silence he sighed. It seemed to Rose that he didn't want to leave but couldn't think of a thing to say.

"Well," Mr. Craig said. He stirred as if he were about to go, but still he held their books in his hands. He looked at Rose and Nate. There was something in his eyes, perhaps a flicker of sadness, that she had never seen before.

"You know, I used to be a schoolteacher before I became a banker," he said.

"Yes sir," said Rose. "I remember."

"I do miss it sometimes," Mr. Craig went on. "Discussing books and stories and great ideas with young people. I would have been proud to have you two children in any of my classes."

"Thank you," said Rose. She wished Mr. Craig would leave.

"I know some stories myself," he said. "Stories I heard from my own family. Would you like to hear one?"

Rose didn't, not for anything. Nate just shrugged. But Rose knew she must be polite to Mr. Craig. "Yes sir," she said. "That would be very kind."

"Well then," Mr. Craig said quickly, "let me see now, which one shall it be?" He picked up the wooden chair, set it by the door, sat down, and crossed his long legs. He pulled at his bony chin for a moment, thinking. "Have you ever heard of a yarbwoman?" he asked brightly.

"I know about that," Nate declared. "A yarbwoman came and caught two babies from Effie. She's my brother's wife."

"Yes, that's right," Mr. Craig said, his eyes smiling. "A yarbwoman is often an old lady who knows all about herbs, about the creatures of the woods, and spells and such. Sometimes they call them granny women."

Then he began to tell the story of the yarb-woman and the rattlesnake.

The Yarbwoman

"Well one time, not so very far from here in the hills, but a long time ago, there lived an old yarbwoman with her granddaughter, Emmy Lou. They lived in an old log house, deep in the forest. The yarbwoman was very old, withered, and small. Emmy Lou was a young girl, only sixteen years old, and she was very beautiful, with long dark braids and deep blue eyes."

Nate slid over and sat next to Rose on the edge of the bed.

"And the yarbwoman, whom Emmy Lou

called Granny, kept a snake. It was a black-snake. Granny didn't like to keep cats, so she had the blacksnake to keep mice from the house. She let that snake have the run of the place. It would curl itself over the rafters, or hide under the floorboards. And sometimes Granny even gave it a little saucer of cow's milk."

Rose stared at Mr. Craig, bewitched by the way his whole person was changing. He leaned forward as he spoke. His hands began to move in the air, his face softened, and his eyes danced with hidden humor.

"Folks around those parts were afraid of Granny. Oh, they came to her in sickness and went away cured by her potions and herbs, but they didn't like that snake. It was said that she could speak with the creatures of the forest, and that she knew spells. They didn't like her one bit, and called her a witch-woman, even though she was the gentlest soul on this earth.

"One day Granny and Emmy Lou had a visit from old Haden Garner, a tall man with a thick, powerful body who lived nearby with his three grown sons. Old Haden was also much feared by the folks in that place. He had a name for mean-spiritedness, and he beat his sons at any excuse. Two of them were as ornery and bad-tempered as their father. They were Big Bill and Hogan.

"The third son, Harrison, was the youngest and a slender weakling among those huge men. He was tenderhearted as well. He hardly spoke, and he sometimes fainted under the thrashing of his cruel father and brothers. In time as he grew up, old Haden, and Big Bill and Hogan, gave up caring about Harrison. At times they even forgot he was there.

"The Garners had no women at home. Poor Mrs. Garner had died some time before, and the men lived almost as animals, never cleaning after themselves, and keeping a shabby house—all except young Harrison, who tried to keep up the place, and even studied his lessons, but only in secret, for if old Haden and his brothers caught him at it, they would just as leave beat or kick him as look at him.

"So when Emmy Lou looked out the door

one morning and saw old Haden coming between the trees, you know that she and Granny were not pleased.

"Old Haden strode into the house and set himself down on a bench by the chimney place, where Granny was simmering a pot of herbs.

"'I am a-wishing speech with you and Emmy Lou,' old Haden said."

Rose's head jerked in surprise. Mr. Craig had suddenly changed his voice, speaking just as a hillman might. It shocked her to hear him talk that way, after weeks and weeks of his polite, proper voice at the dining table.

"Granny just kept stirring her pot of herbs.

"'I was up along to the county seat two weeks ago,' Haden told her," Mr. Craig continued. "'It 'pears by law that this here land on which your cabin stands rightly belongs to me.'

"Now Granny had already heard about it, so she just kept stirring that pot.

"'You-all hold nary title to it,' old Haden Garner told her. 'By law and title, all the land on this here side of the creek, it belongs to me.'

"Emmy Lou couldn't hold her tongue. She cried out, 'But when Granny was a young thing, the creek run on t'other side of the house from what it does now.'

"'Law takes nary account of the creek's wanderings,' old Haden said. 'I hold title to the creek's edge. I took a lawyer's advice on it.'

"Poor Emmy Lou was so upset, she couldn't speak. And then Haden Garner said to Granny, 'I ain't a-aiming to take nary advantage of the fact. What I aim to do is wed Emmy Lou. I am a widow-man. I have need of a woman in my house. I reckon she will suit me mighty well. As for you, Granny, I will give you leave to live in this house 'til your dyin' day.'

"And Haden stood up and began to walk out the door. But he shied at the last moment, startled by the blacksnake, which hung down from one the rafters. He snatched a grubbing hoe that was by the door and was about to kill that snake when Granny finally spoke.

"'Lay nary hand upon him,' she growled. ''Tis but a harmless, gentle creature that stays by us and hunts for mice. Lay nary hand upon him.'"

Mr. Craig made his voice low and gravelly. A shiver crept up Rose's spine.

"And Haden Garner left that house, telling Granny that he would wed poor Emmy Lou in two weeks' time, when the circuit rider would be along. Otherwise, the two women would be put out of their house and land."

"What's a circuit rider?" Rose asked.

"A traveling judge," said Mr. Craig.

"Now poor Emmy Lou was beside herself with grief. What could they do against such a powerful man?

"'I hate and despise him,' she told Granny. 'From the bottom of my soul.'

"'Don't wed him,' Granny said. She began to hum a song to the snake, and it slithered its way down the grubbing hoe and across the floor, its tongue flickering like a tiny bit of lightning, to where Granny sat.

"'But Granny, where will we go, without a place to sleep, and nary true friend to take us in?'

"Granny stared into the dying coals of the fire for a long time, holding her knees in her thin arms. Finally she said, 'I am old, and little life remains in my body, but I am not afeared, and don't you be. The wild creatures will watch over us. There's many things beyond your understanding that's well known to me.' "

"Gosh," Nate breathed. "What happened?"

"Well, old Haden talked bold when he got home to his sons. Granny would give up Emmy Lou, he was sure of that. He and his older sons began to plan a big wedding frolic.

"One day, about a week later, he decided to go and pay a visit to Emmy Lou. He wanted the poor girl to come and redd up his house, to make it clean and tidy for the frolic.

"Over his bare feet he put on a pair of boots that belonged to his son Hogan. They were the only boots in the house, and all the men took turns wearing them when they wanted.

"He got down to the river and stumbled on a big rattlesnake. It struck him, through the thin leather of the upper boot, right into his leg. He smashed the head of it with the stock of his rifle, but it was too late.

"He hobbled back to the house with the dead snake, calling out to his sons for whiskey, which the old-timers thought was a cure for snakebite. And they cut that snake up, opened the wound with a knife, and tried to draw out the poison by holding the bits of snakemeat against his leg.

"Then they carried him inside, and soon he fell asleep, his leg all blown up with poison. But they could see he wasn't going to die. Old Haden was a big, strong man; not even a rattlesnake could kill him.

"The boys fell to talking. Hogan was nervous. He remembered a story about a child who had seen a yarbwoman turn herself into a snake. 'I reckon it's naught but idle talk,' he said. But the others could see he was worried.

"Big Bill just laughed, looking at the shattered body of the rattlesnake. 'If that yarbwoman took the body of that snake, I reckon there's but little left of her now.'

"Well, the next morning Haden woke up, feeling awful, but as determined as ever. He told Hogan, 'You go tell that yarbwoman's gal I aim to wed come Saturday. There's nary woman alive can best Haden Garner. If she's a-scheming otherwise, her and her old witch-granny can get out of my house and off my land afore tomorrow eve.'

"Hogan didn't want to go, but Haden browbeat him to do it, and Big Bill laughed and called him a white-livered belly-crawler. So he had to go, to save his face.

"Hogan put on the boots and he left. Haden and Big Bill fell asleep. Harrison sneaked his arithmetic lessons by the light of a pine knot on the hearth. He wanted to be a schoolteacher, for he was not big enough to be a woodcutter like his brothers. But he could study his lessons only when his brothers were asleep or away.

"Suddenly Hogan stumbled through the door, waking up Haden and Big Bill. He was pulling hard at his boot. 'I cain't get it off,' he nearly cried. 'I'm a-feeling mighty poorly. I reckon I'm snakebit,' he wailed. 'She's witched me! I'm doomed!'

"Young Harrison pulled off Hogan's boot and looked at his leg. It was swollen up, but he could find no tooth marks of a snake, only some briar scratches and chigger bites.

" 'Where'd it bite you?' he asked Hogan.

" 'I never seen no snake,' Hogan answered. He talked with a thick tongue now, and he swayed dizzily. 'It was the snake-woman, I tell you. I went, and you said there'd be but little left of her,' he told Big Bill. 'But there she lay, under her covers, a-speaking nary word, just a-fixing me with her evil eye. Her head's all bound up in a cloth. Emmy Lou, she'll never wed you' was the last thing he said to old Haden before he fell unconscious.

"By next morning, Hogan was dead."

Mr. Craig stopped speaking for a moment. He recrossed his legs and cleared his throat. Just then a passing train let out a fierce whistle, and Rose felt Nate's body jump next to her. Her own heart was beating fast.

"Well, by nightfall every soul in those hills had heard these facts. When folks came to Hogan's funeral, they wouldn't pass by the yarbwoman's house, except a few brave and curious souls who went by in daylight and said the place was deserted, except for a little smoke from the chimney.

"They started talking against Emmy Lou's

granny, hating her the way people hate snakes. They were terrified.

"But Big Bill didn't believe in spells. He told Haden that Emmy Lou must have given Hogan a drink of water that had been poisoned. He worked himself into a terrible fury.

" 'If there's witch's work in it, leave her try it once on Big Bill. I ain't afeared!' He grabbed his gun and pulled on Hogan's boots, and off he went to Granny's house.

"When morning came, and Big Bill was not home, Harrison and Haden went out to look for him. They gathered up a group of men. They searched and searched all that day and all that night, but he was nowhere to be found.

"Mean old Haden became crazier and crazier. Finally he turned on his last son, Harrison, like a man gone mad.

" 'I know what you're a-thinking!' he shouted. 'You're a-thinking to heir my property. You're aiming to stand in dead men's shoes, but nary smitch of it will be yours.' He raised his gun to shoot Harrison, but the other men stopped him.

" 'Leave me catch a glimpse of you once

more, and I'll kill you!' he cried out. Harrison went quickly down the road. He knew now that he had nowhere else to go, but he wanted to have his schoolbooks, which were hidden under the kitchen-house.

"He wandered through the woods, thinking what to do. Finally he came to a spring and was about to go down to it to drink when he saw Emmy Lou, holding a gourd dipper. He wasn't afraid of Emmy Lou, or her granny. And his heart was taken over by her beauty. 'I was a-craving a drink,' Harrison said to her.

"She handed him the dipper and he drank, looking at her pure young face. 'I reckon you been a-seeking Big Bill Garner,' she said.

"'Yes, I been a-seeking him,' said Harrison. 'Folks say he was aiming to come to your place.'

"'He never,' Emmy Lou said loudly. 'No, he never.'

"Then she walked quickly away and Harrison made to follow her. But she turned on him. 'Don't you come nigh us,' she warned him, and ran off to Granny's house.

"The next day they found Hogan's boots,

the ones Big Bill was wearing. And a little way off, they found Big Bill, dead, with his leg badly swollen.

"Old Haden had not slept in days, and now he raged like a beast driven by terror. He put on Hogan's boots and got together a big crowd of neighboring men to go deal with Granny. Not a one among them thought she didn't have something to do with the deaths of Hogan and Big Bill. And they had guns.

"Young Harrison heard about it, and he hurried ahead to Granny's house, with a shotgun he had sneaked out of his father's house, to warn Emmy Lou.

"Poor Emmy Lou was just about scared out of her wits. So was gentle Harrison, but he wouldn't let Emmy Lou see his fear. She begged him to go away. 'They'll kill you,' she said.

"But Harrison wouldn't go. He was lonesome, and he could see that Emmy Lou was lonesome too. So together they sat there on the porch in the moonlight, with Granny asleep in her bed, talking quietly, giving each other courage. And Harrison swore to Emmy Lou that if they lived to see daylight, he would stay by her and protect her and Granny forever.

"'I know your granny ain't no witch-woman,' he told her. 'There's a natural explanation for everything, as surely as four times four is sixteen.'

"Well, along about daylight the crowd of men finally came, thirty of them, with Haden at the front. They all had guns, and coal oil too, to burn down Granny's house.

"Harrison sent Emmy Lou inside. When Haden saw his boy Harrison on the porch, he stopped short and rose up in righteous fury. 'Are you in league with that there yarb-woman?' he demanded, raising his rifle. 'Leave us have her! Stand back or—'

"But those were the last words Haden Garner ever spoke. He dropped his rifle, grabbed at his throat, and screamed. He tried to speak but couldn't. He fell to the ground, wriggling and writhing like a man possessed.

"The others rushed to his side. Haden pointed to his leg. It was swollen up inside the boot. They cut the boot away, but there was no mark of a snakebite on his leg anywhere.

"Old Haden moaned once and died, right on the spot."

Nate grabbed Rose's arm so suddenly, she jumped with fright. Mr. Craig smiled but pressed on.

"That riled up the crowd of men. 'Murderer,' they cried out, and began to pour coal oil on the porch. Granny came out and begged Harrison to let them take her, to spare poor Emmy Lou. But Harrison wouldn't hear of it.

"A pine torch was brought up, and they were just about to set the place afire when one of the men who had pulled off old Haden's boot cried out, 'I see it! I see it plain! Lookit here!'

"He had the boot in his hand, and now he spread it open, pointing.

"'There's the rattler's fang. Look!'

"And sure enough, when the men crowded around, they could see that the fang of the snake Haden had killed was still stuck in the leather. It was the same boot that Hogan had worn, and Big Bill after him, and Haden again on the last night of his life.

"That same fang had killed them all. Every time they wore those same boots, the fang bit them. Now everyone saw for their own eyes that Granny was no witch-woman. Gentle Harrison married Emmy Lou, and he gave Granny her land and house, free and clear."

Mr. Craig sat back and folded his arms, grinning.

Rose was speechless. It was such a wonderful story. She had never guessed about the boot, and the way Mr. Craig told it, she could see everything clearly in her mind's eye. But she was most amazed that stuffy Mr. Craig had that story inside him. Rose would never have said it was possible.

"Phew!" Nate cried out, throwing himself backward on the bed. "Phew! That's the best story I ever heard. Ever!"

"What's all this commotion?" Mama's voice called out from the parlor. Mr. Craig sprang to his feet and pulled his vest smooth. His face went stone sober, and he looked about as if searching for a place to run.

Mama's quick steps tapped across the floor. "I've told you to mind your voices when Mr. Craig is . . . Oh, hello, Mr. Craig," she said, pulling off her gloves one finger at a time. "I'm terribly sorry if the children have been disturbing you. If I have told them once I have told them a hundred times . . ."

"It is entirely my fault," Mr. Craig interrupted. "I was just telling them a foolish story I heard as a youngster. I'm sorry that I have gotten them all riled up. If you'll excuse me, I think I'll take a short nap before supper."

Mama watched him go, a quizzical look on her face.

Rose sat there stunned for a long moment. She was completely perplexed by Mr. Craig. It was true what people said: You couldn't ever tell a book by the cover.

War!

The winter flew by in a blur of steaming pots, dirty dishes, laundered sheets, spelldowns, visits to the farm, social calls, and always, always, the yearning cries of the passing trains.

Over the months of living in town, the rhythm of the trains had become as natural and comforting to Rose as the rising and setting of the sun. If a bad snowstorm or a flood down the line had blocked the track, her ears strained for the sound of a whistle but heard only the strange and troubling silence of the wind moaning in the wires. That was the silence of a stopped clock.

When the first train finally got through, everyone commented on it, breathed a little sigh of contentment, and went back to the chores.

Rose had gotten to know the faces of many of the engineers. Some of them ignored her when she waved; some even scowled. A few waved back.

She especially looked forward to the eastbound local, Number 105. It came through at 3:20 in the afternoon. Rose knew the schedule by heart. Number 105 passed by after the dreadful boredom of schoolwork was over and before the supper chores had begun. That was a time for Rose to have some moments to herself, before Mama called her to bring in the stove wood.

After she walked down the hill from school, she usually visited Bunting in the barn and played a game of fetch with Fido. And always when Number 105 passed, the engineer leaned out of his cab and waved to Rose. Then he hooted his horn once, just for her.

It was odd to wave every day to a person she hadn't met, whose name she didn't know. Yet she would run home from school, if she had dawdled to talk to someone or play a game, so she wouldn't miss Number 105. That man, with his big grin under his striped cap and his waving hand covered with a heavy cuffed glove, made her feel part of the rushing trains.

He was always hurrying somewhere, to faraway places Rose could only read about in books. He looked out his window at hundreds and hundreds of miles of farms and towns and great cities. Rose thought surely there were thousands of children to wave to, yet he always remembered her, and that made her feel important, like the trains.

Someday she knew she would ride on one, and see the places she had read about and many she had never imagined. Sitting on the barn lot fence, Rose decided a train was like a book, a story that started here and ended there, and in between was full of excitement, adventure, and comfort.

There was more traffic on the rails now. Extra freight trains pulled flat cars loaded with great earth-moving machines, stacks of rails, and piles of cross ties. Then came more freights pulling cars loaded with stone for the rail bed.

On the road in front of the house, there were more wagons, too, bringing more cross ties that farmers and woodsmen had hacked out of the forests.

Abe and Papa sold many wagonloads of cross ties, and beams for building bridges over creeks, too. Papa said things were looking up. Mama had her bed and board money, and there was so much freight coming in and out of town that some days Papa hired an extra wagon and team from Hoover's Livery and paid Paul to skip school and drive it. And they still had Mama's egg and butter money.

"We're taking in cash money with both hands," Papa crowed. "We've already made up for the loss of last year's crops. Taxes are paid, the mortgage is current, and we even have a few dollars in the bank. Looks as if our luck has finally turned, Bess."

"Diligence is the mother of good luck," said Mama, huffing as she kneaded a big wad of bread dough on the kitchen table. "It's hard work that will get us where we want to go. And I won't relax until the farm is paid off."

Next the trains brought grading crews who came to set up the equipment to be ready for the spring thaw. Then they would set to work, grinding down the slopes and building up the hollows to make a good level road for the rails to Ava.

The trains brought news as well. One warm afternoon after school, during the first thaw, Papa came rushing into the kitchen without scraping his boots, startling Rose and Mama from their mending.

"You won't believe what's happened!" he gasped. "Just came over the telegraph at the depot. Those treacherous Spaniards have sunk one of our battleships in Cuba."

"Sunk an American ship?" Mama asked in wonderment. "But whatever for? The newspapers have been saying for months that the Spanish have stopped mistreating the Cubans, and practically given them their freedom."

"They're a pack of sly dogs," Papa said angrily, a red flag of rage flying on each cheek.

"They must have sneaked a bomb on board. Blew our ship up at anchor, and she sank in minutes. Just think of it, hundreds of good American boys killed or drowned."

"Oh, Manly. That's horrible!" Mama's forehead knotted up. "Oh, I hope those fools in Washington . . . You don't think . . ."

"I think exactly that," Papa interrupted. "Mark my words, Bess. President McKinley can talk peace 'til he's blue in the face. No American is going to sit on his hands while our sailors are murdered in their beds. We're going to war!"

A clamor slowly rose across the whole town as the news spread. The school bell began to ring, and in town, the fire bell tolled. Rose ran to the parlor and looked out the window. Men and boys were running toward the square, pulling on their coats and hats and shouting hoarsely.

Rose's scalp crinkled with fear. War! Just the sound of the word chilled her to the bone. It was terrifying the way the town had suddenly erupted in noisy outrage.

The furor continued all that day, and into the evening, except for a lull at suppertime.

Everything stopped, except for the trains. Papa put up his draywagon and the mares at Hoover's Livery and was gone for long spells, coming back to bring the latest news from the telegraph office.

He said the ship was called the *Maine* and it was one of the finest in the American navy. The bomb had exploded at night, when the poor sailors were asleep in their bunks and couldn't escape. The president had made a speech asking all Americans to hold their opinions until all the facts could be known. But Papa said the people had already made their opinions and the folks in town were getting up a rally to support it: Spain must be made to pay.

Rose desperately wanted to go uptown with him to see, but Mama wouldn't hear of it.

"I can just imagine what's going on up there at the depot, and two saloons just across the street. Get a bunch of men stirred up, and Lord knows what kind of mischief will come of it."

"Why?" Rose wondered. "Why did the Spanish blow up the ship?"

Mama sighed wearily. "Who can say? The

Cuban people have been fighting against the Spanish for a long time, to have their freedom, just as we Americans fought to make the British leave.

"Cuba is very close to Florida, so President McKinley had sent our ships to show the colors in friendship with Spain. It doesn't make a bit of sense, the Spaniards sinking our ship. I wouldn't wonder if it were the Cubans."

"Will there really be a war?" Rose worried.

"McKinley promised to keep us out of any wars. But after this, I wonder if he can."

At supper Papa, the railroad men, and Mr. Craig talked loudly and forcefully about the sinking of the *Maine*, and what the future might hold. Rose and Mama didn't have to lean from their kitchen chairs. They could hear every word.

"If you ask me, it's about time we threw the Spanish out of there and showed the world that the Monroe Doctrine isn't just a scrap of paper," one of the railroad men said. "The very idea, thinking they can still bully the little peoples of the world. The Western Hemisphere belongs to the Americans now, to the folks that settled them, not to a gang of thieves hiding behind their thrones in Europe."

"I don't entirely disagree with you," Mr. Craig said. "But I wonder what place we have mucking around in the affairs of others. If Cuba is meant to belong to the Cubans, they will make it so. The American colonials did it here. It took years of hardship, but we did it."

"But Craig, you must see the point that we have our interests to guard," Papa chimed in. "Until the question of Cuba is settled, Spain is a thorn in our side, with Cuba just a hundred miles or so off the coast of Florida. If we don't stop them in Cuba, who's to say Spain or some other power won't try to muscle their way into our trading routes? I reckon Germany and France would like nothing better than to get their hands on the Caribbean islands."

"It's a question of principle," said the other railroad man. "The United States stands for freedom and liberty, wherever folks are fighting for it."

Rose's head spun from trying to keep up

with that argument. She didn't know what to think.

Supper was over in a wink, and then the men dashed back uptown. That night when Rose went outside to toss the dirty dishwater out by the barn lot, she could see flickering lights and shadows on the wall of the grain mill, and hear the roar of men's voices chanting and cheering by the depot.

There was no school the next day, in honor of the sailors who had died. At dinner Papa brought home a stack of newspapers brought by the trains. Nearly every column was filled with stories of the tragic sinking of the *Maine*, and the clamor all across the country for revenge.

Season of Hope

The muddy ground froze hard again and rivers of gray clouds flowed across the cold sky. Winter clung stubbornly to the Ozark hills, and so did talk of the sinking of the *Maine*.

Mrs. Honeycutt made a geography lesson of it one day. She brought to school a borrowed globe of the earth and told how the great kingdoms of Europe had once ruled much of the world. She said all that was changing. Now even the smallest country cried out for its freedom.

Rose remembered Mama's talk at the debate

and thought of the Indians crying out for their freedom, too. She wondered how it could be that America would help the Cubans but fight the Indians. Wasn't America their country before it was everyone else's?

"I'll go fight those Spanish," Nate declared to the room, "and show 'em who's boss." Many of the other boys piped up that they would, too.

"I certainly hope you never have to," Mrs. Honeycutt said. "For war is a terrible thing. It may seem adventurous and heroic to you, sitting here in our warm, cozy schoolroom."

Then her voice became earnest. "But war is not just a story in a book. It is another matter to be in battle, to be shot at and hurt and to see your fellow soldiers hurt and even killed.

"You children are too young to know about the Civil War, when brother fought against brother. But you will understand when you are grown-up. War is a waste of life and a feast for vultures."

The scholars fell quiet and sober after that. Rose remembered her favorite poem, about the charge of the Light Brigade, which rode into the Valley of Death. She did not want there to be a war with Spain, or with anyone, ever. She did not want Nate or Paul or any boy to die fighting for someone else's freedom.

In that moment, Rose suddenly realized that she had made up her own mind about a war with Spain. She had heard about the horrible torturings and beatings of the Cubans by their Spanish masters.

She wanted the Cubans to live free, but she believed they should fight for it themselves. She remembered that Mama never liked to be beholden to people. "Who accepts from another sells his freedom," she had said.

From her history lessons she remembered what Patrick Henry had said when Americans fought for their freedom. He said, "Give me liberty, or give me death." That was the choice of the Cubans, to make for themselves.

In time, people talked less and less of Cuba. Spring was coming, and with it the chores of preparing the land and seeding it. Work pushed

out thoughts of faraway places and rumors of war.

As soon as the ground had thawed enough, Papa hauled the plow from the farm and made a garden bed for Mama next to the barn lot in the backyard. Mama kept Rose home from the last weeks of school to help with the hoeing and planting.

Spring always brought hard work, but it was work Rose enjoyed. She didn't like the harvest season, when the birds had flown south and the earth was going to sleep. Harvesting was the season of worry, when the crops must be gotten in before the frost could kill them.

Spring was filled with hope: that the tiny fragile seeds would sprout and grow strong; that it would rain enough but not too much; and that all their crops would bear a rich harvest.

The farm needed tending as well. The Bairds could not do it all by themselves, with two babies to watch. On some days Papa, Rose, and Mama went out to Rocky Ridge, to help with Effie's garden. Papa helped Abe and Nate with the plowing, mending fences, white-washing the orchard tree trunks, and planting corn, pumpkins, squash, and sorghum.

It was a relief from the soiled muddy streets and noise of town to be out in the country again, leading Bunting to pasture, hunting for fresh greens, and listening for the first war-blings of the returning summer birds.

One Saturday, when Rose was helping Mama plant the potatoes back in town, Mrs. Cooley came by with Paul and an apple pie.

"Our apples had just about gone all mealy, so I baked them up into pies," Mrs. Cooley told Mama. "I made so many, we could never finish them all. I thought you might like one, although I had to sweeten them quite a bit."

Mama and Mrs. Cooley went into the house to visit. Paul stood leaning his elbow on the hoe handle, watching Rose as she knelt at her work. Thick fluffy clouds sailed across the sky, and the sun lay on Rose's shoulders like a warm blanket.

A little wren sang her heart out in the sycamore tree near the privy. Next door the

Gaskill children were screaming with pleasure as they pushed each other on their swing. The Hardestys were out, too, painting their barn with a fresh coat of red.

All around them were the sounds of hammering and sawing. Spring in town was a time of building and repairing.

"You should come out sometime with your papa and see them putting in the railroad bed," Paul said. "Especially when they dynamite the rocks. It's something to watch."

"I would like that," said Rose, digging a hole in the mound of soft earth and pushing a seed potato into it. "But there's so much hoeing and planting to be done, and keeping house and cooking. I hardly have time even to read."

Rose covered up the little lump of seed potato and dug another hole for the next one. It felt good to sink her fingers into the dirt and smell the rich scent of it. "We're going out to the farm tomorrow, after church. You could come. Maybe the apple trees will be in bloom. They're getting to be so big now."

"Sure," Paul said, batting at a curious bee

with his hat. "That would be swell. Gosh, Rose, do you think there's to be a war? Everyone says it's as sure as rain."

"I would hate it if there was," said Rose. "Mrs. Honeycutt says war is a feast for vultures."

"Well, I wouldn't go if there was. I couldn't ever leave Mama alone with George. He's too foolish to care for her, and I've got work now. That's cash money we need to keep up the house."

They chattered a long time, until finally Mama and Mrs. Cooley came out of the house, and Paul went home with his mother.

The next day Rose walked with Mama and Papa to church—down the street toward town, past the livery stable, along the block of closed stores that faced the square, across the railroad tracks, and up the slope to the church.

They sat where Mama always wanted to sit, halfway between the pulpit and the door. That was where most of the families sat. Blanche and her mother and father sat in the middle as well, and Mrs. Cooley, and the Beaumonts, who drove to church in a beautiful brass-trimmed buggy.

The bald heads and old-fashioned bonnets of the old people perched in the rows in front of them. Behind the families were the young ladies who were old enough to sit with their beaux. In the back, Paul and George and Blanche's brothers sat with the other boys, twisting and turning, joking, and making their stealthy disturbances.

Rose thought church was always interesting. She got to see everyone's best clothes, and to listen to the whispered bits of gossip about any young lady who had come with a new beau, or without an old one. Church always gave people something to talk about through the next week.

That morning the young doctor came to church. He was old Dr. Padgett's nephew, but nobody knew him yet. He had worked as a hand on his father's farm, Rose heard Mama whisper to Papa. One day, working in the corn- field, he'd laid down his grubbing hoe and said he'd not hoe another row. He had gone to school to become a doctor, and somehow he'd done it.

Everyone in church looked at him now. He still had his country air. His sleeves were too short, and he tugged at his collar. It made church interesting to look at him, and see all the young ladies pretending not to notice him at all.

When church ended, there was always a confused crowding as everyone shuffled down the aisle toward the back. A shaft of sunlight came through the open doors. The Beaumonts were in front of Rose, and Papa and Mama were behind her as they inched forward.

Rose craned to see if she could spy Paul. Maybe he would come home with them to dinner, and then ride out to the farm. Finally Rose reached the doorsill, and she could see over the heads of the Beaumonts as they went down the steps.

Along either side of the walkway, boys were jostling and jeering. The men hurried to their teams and buggies and wagons; the women nudged and murmured. All in one moment Rose saw Paul, standing among the boys, quickly take off his hat, step forward, and whisper to Lois Beaumont.

Rose stood rooted to the floorboards, too shocked to move. Her heart skipped a beat. Lois turned and looked hopefully at her mother and father. Her mother nodded her head. Then Lois placed a gloved hand on Paul's arm, and together they walked down the path.

Rose watched them go, her thoughts jumping about like rabbits. Then she felt a hand on her arm, and Mama's voice, "Come along, now. You're blocking the way."

Rose nearly stumbled going down the stairs. She couldn't tear her eyes from the backs of Paul and Lois, walking close together, in the procession of groups and couples making their way down the slope, across the tracks, and along the sidewalk by the square.

Her heart beat wildly. She almost had to gasp to get her breath. At the corner of the square Paul and Lois, followed now by Mr. and Mrs. Beaumont driving slowly in their buggy, turned left and headed west, toward the Beaumonts' mansion.

She realized, with a horrible sinking feeling, that Paul was sparking with Lois Beaumont, beautiful Lois with her perfect golden hair, her fashionable dress, and her feathered hat. Rose's chest tightened painfully. Her mind went black with a rage that shimmered hotly on her skin.

When they reached the corner of the square, Mama had to call her twice to come along.

"What in the world are you gawking at?" she asked. "Didn't you hear me?"

Changing Fast

Mama and Papa stopped to speak with Mrs. Rippee on the street. Rose couldn't bear to be around people. She wanted to go off and be by herself, so she ran the rest of the way home. She burst through the front door and slammed it so hard behind her that a railroad chromolithograph of Niagara Falls that hung on the wall clattered to the floor.

She didn't care how much noise she made. Anyway, Mr. Craig was away for the weekend visiting his family, and the railroad men had gone to Springfield for business.

She stormed through the house, into the bedroom, and clambered up the ladder to her attic room. She kicked off her shoes so hard, they hit the sloped ceiling. Then she threw herself down on her bed and hugged her hurt to herself in silent grief. Hot, unshed tears quivered in her eyes.

Rose's heart filled with poison. She hated Lois, just hated everything about her: her fancy airs, her easy smile, even the way she jingled her bracelet when she talked.

It was harder to hate Paul, but she wanted to, desperately. How could he be so cruel? How could he like someone like Lois?

Rose lay there in a pool of misery, thinking a stream of wicked, hateful thoughts until she heard Mama and Papa come into the house. She couldn't go downstairs, not for anything. She couldn't be seen as stirred up as a cyclone.

"Rose," Mama's voice called out from the kitchen.

"I'm up here," Rose croaked.

"Papa and I are going up to the Helfinstines' for a small visit before dinner. Be a good girl and put some more wood in the stove, and set the pot on to warm."

"Yes, Mama," Rose called back.

The door latched, and the house fell silent. She listened to the sounds of wagons and buggies rumbling up and down the street. The wren was singing again, but its trilling notes were tinged with sadness. Life was still going on, but it seemed to be far away and ghostly, as in a dream.

Slowly Rose pulled herself up and sat drooping on the edge of her bed. She felt drained and hollow. Her body ached feverishly. Finally she climbed down the ladder. She was about to go into the kitchen when she stopped in front of the chifforobe.

She slowly opened the door and looked shyly, sideways, stealing a glance, into the mirror. Rose looked back at herself with the pained eyes of a scolded dog. Her new lawn dress was wrinkled and rumpled from lying in it. The sash had slipped on one side and hung loose and crooked from her waist.

Rose pulled at the yoke of her dress to puff

it out and see what she might look like as a grown woman. When she let go, the cloth fell right back into its smooth place on her chest. She sighed heavily.

Then Rose began to look at all of herself, head to toe. It made her blood run cold. Standing in that mirror was a short, squat girl with dull gray eyes, mousy brown hair, fat cheeks, and nails chipped from housework and gardening. She saw a girl who could never be as beautiful and perfectly dressed and graceful as Lois Beaumont. She saw a girl whom Paul would never ask to let him walk her home from church.

Rose began to sob. It started with one great sob that grabbed her whole being like a giant fist and squeezed so tightly that she had to double over. Every muscle in her body cried out, then a gasp and another fist, and another, and another. The sound coming from her mouth, a wounded animal's low moan, scared her, but she couldn't stop it.

She cried and cried and cried, until she was sure she had used up her last tear. And then she cried some more and crumpled to the floor.

That was how Mama found her when she and Papa came home from the Helfinstines'. Mama was frantic with worry at first, checking her arms and legs to see if she had fallen off the ladder.

When Rose shook her head, no, she wasn't hurt, Mama gathered her up in her arms and sat with her on the edge of the big bed, just rocking her while Rose cried out the rest of her tears. Papa stuck his head in, but Mama waved him away.

It took Rose a long, long time to calm herself and catch her breath. She was exhausted from sobbing. Her damp dress clung to her prickly skin, and Mama's handkerchief was soaked. It took every ounce of her strength to explain herself. She was hiccupping and couldn't look at Mama, she was so embarrassed and ashamed.

Mama listened quietly, stirring only once, to reach over and push closed the chifforobe door.

When Rose had talked herself out, she finally raised her head and looked into Mama's face. Mama's blue eyes shimmered brightly, and she looked at Rose with the tenderness of a new mother.

Her first words brought a new flood to Rose's eyes, but those were cleansing tears.

"I love you," she said. She leaned forward and planted a kiss on Rose's forehead. "Just the way you are."

"I know," Rose said with a snuffle. "But that doesn't change a thing. I'm still plain."

"Do you think I am plain?" Mama asked.

"You're beautiful," said Rose. "Anyone can see it."

"I'm glad you think so, because you are my flesh and blood, and you look quite a bit as I did at your age."

"I d-do?" Rose said in surprise. "You were plain then?"

"Plain as pudding," Mama chuckled. "I hated my hair, because it wasn't golden like your aunt Mary's. I was so squat that your grandpa Ingalls called me Half-pint, and said I was built like a little French horse. How would you like to be compared to a stubby old thing like that?"

A smile crept onto Rose's lips. "I wouldn't."

"Grandpa didn't mean to be unkind. He was just trying to cheer me up because I didn't like my looks. But then I grew up and no one seemed to notice anymore the things I didn't like about myself, certainly not your father."

"You mean I won't be plain forever?" Rose asked hopefully.

"You are anything but plain now, Rose," Mama said comfortingly, patting down a stray hair on Rose's head. "You are just young, and changing fast, too. One day when you look in the mirror, you won't see the person you see today. There will be a beautiful young girl any boy'd be glad to walk home."

Rose thought about that for a quiet moment. People do change when they grow up. Paul had changed from a boy to almost a man. Chubby kittens became sleek cats, and awkward colts grew into graceful horses.

Then she remembered Lois. "But Paul likes Lois now," she began to whine. "It'll be forever before I grow up."

Mama shushed her. "Listen to me. You will

grow up soon enough, and if it is meant to be that Paul likes you back one day, there is time enough for that. You may be growing up fast, Rose, but you are a long way from grown up. You're too young to be worrying yourself about such things.

"As for Lois Beaumont, I know that kind of girl. I know the kind of boy Paul is. He's good, and loyal, and too smart to have his head turned by a rich girl putting on airs. He's young, too. He has not finished his growing up, and I think they will tire of each other soon enough. Time will tell the truth.

"It's the most natural thing for boys to want to walk girls home from church. But it often doesn't mean a thing."

Rose felt a little better after that, but she still dragged herself through dinner and washing up. For once, Mama didn't chide her to hurry.

After dinner they drove out to the farm. As the team pulled up the hill to the barnyard, Rose was shocked to see Paul standing on the porch talking with Abe.

Paul was friendly as ever to her, but Rose felt

clumsy and small, and she struggled to think of things to talk about. They went for a walk in the orchard. The blossoms were just opening, and the air hummed with the buzzing of bees. Here and there lay little piles of ashes where Abe had lit fires on the night of a late frost to keep the buds from freezing. The white-washed trunks of the rows of trees looked like freshly painted fences. The air was sweet, and the strong sunshine filtered along the branches.

Paul talked about the Beaumonts' beautiful mansion with its columned porch, and Mr. Beaumont's fine buggy and team. Rose had to swallow her words and listen as if she didn't care one way or the other, but inside she ached.

That next week, one morning after the dishes were washed and the floors swept, Mama said, "Put on your second-best dress. There's something I need from Reynolds', and I want you to come with me."

They walked uptown through the spring mud, Mama holding up the hem of her skirt to keep it from getting dirty. A soft, gentle rain fell, forming little droplets of mist on their cold noses. They huddled against the chill in their coats, but this weather was good for the gardens and crops.

Inside the store they shook off the dampness like sparrows. It was warm and cozy in there, with the big potbellied stove crackling and the air thick with the smells of leather and coal oil and pickle brine.

Mama marched straight over to the counter of cloth goods. Rose was surprised. They had already made up their summer lawns, and Papa had a new pair of overalls and two new chambray shirts.

"Mornin', Mrs. Wilder," said the clerk. "What can we show you today?"

"My husband tells me you have got in some new silks. I would like to see them."

"Yes, ma'am," he said. "I was just putting them out, in fact." He turned around and pulled out a pile of plump bolts from the shelves behind him.

He piled them all out on the counter, folding the cut end of each one over so Mama could see both sides of the cloth. All those bolts together made a gleaming rainbow with the light running all through the shimmering threads.

"Mama, what . . . ?" Rose began to ask, but Mama interrupted her.

"I expect it's high time you had something fancy to wear. How do you like these surah silks? I thought a plain colored skirt would look well, with a lace hem. I could make up a shirt-waist to go with it."

Rose was speechless with shock and delight. She ran her hand over the smooth, fresh cloth in every color imaginable: navy, green, brown, yellow, purple, myrtle. A skirt! In silk! It was too wonderful to believe. She had never had a skirt, and a shirtwaist was something big girls and grown-up ladies wore.

"Oh, Mama," Rose whispered. "The colors are so lively. I like them all."

Mama chuckled. "Well, we must pick one. The navy is very rich-looking, and practical, too. It won't show soiling as much."

Rose touched every bolt. She was overwhelmed with indecision. Each one would be perfect in its own way. But of them all, the red simply vibrated with color. "I like this one," she said.

"Mmmm." Mama thought. "It is very vigorous. Red is a good trimming color, but a whole skirt of it would surely be too bold. The myrtle is pretty. See, it has a bluish tinge to it."

Rose didn't want a dark color. She wanted something bright. So after a long time of thinking, she picked heliotrope. It was lavender, with a reddish blush.

"That will go well with your eyes," Mama said.

She bought three yards, and some snowy linen to make the shirtwaist. She would buy the lace when the skirt and waist were sewn up.

Rose could have skipped all the way home, if the street and sidewalks hadn't been so muddy. Mama and Rose worked together on the skirt, between meals, housework, and garden chores. Mama measured Rose's waist, cut the silk, and basted the panels together. Then Rose sat at the kitchen table putting in the perfect, tiny stitches of the seams the way Mama had taught her.

Mama worked on the shirtwaist by herself, because it had to fit just so, and she wanted to put an extra hem in the sleeves and the yoke to leave room to let it out as Rose got bigger.

She was so looking forward to wearing it that Rose even took her sewing to bed at night, sitting cross-legged on the straw tick with the oil lamp on her dresser purring softly. She stitched and stitched until her neck became stiff, her fingers ached, and she couldn't hold her eyes open anymore.

"For heaven's sake, Rose, put out the light and go to sleep," Mama called up. "You'll ruin your eyes, and it's a waste of coal oil."

Some nights Rose grew so weary, she laid her work down at the foot of the bed and fell asleep in her clothes.

It took two whole weeks to finish everything, including a lace hem in the skirt, and lace on the cuffs and collar of the waist. But when it was done, Rose thought that it was the prettiest outfit she'd ever seen and that it looked very grown-up on her, like the pictures of Gibson girls she'd seen in magazines.

She especially liked the way the waist cinched at her hips, and blossomed out around her shoulders and arms. When she turned, the slippery silk of the skirt whispered and swished around her legs like flowing water.

Then Mama surprised her again with a boater, a straw hat with a wide brim. She had sewn a ribbon of the heliotrope on it, and tied it into a bow at the back. Now when she looked in the mirror, Rose saw something completely new: a pretty, almost grown-up girl who could hold her head up high as she walked down the sidewalk to church on Sunday.

She knew she was still short and that her cheeks were still babyish, but she didn't think much about it anymore. When Mrs. Rippee and even Blanche passed a compliment on her new outfit, she glowed with pleasure.

The American Empire

War was on everyone's lips again. The Congress in Washington, D.C., had voted to spend fifty million dollars to send soldiers and ships to fight Spain. Mama was spitting mad as she sat in the kitchen reading about it in the *Chicago InterOcean*. Rose stood reading over her shoulder.

Through the open dining-room door, she could see Papa and Mr. Craig finishing their coffee.

"Remember the *Maine*!" one headline screamed.

"Fifty million dollars!" Mama fumed, rattling

the page. "Imagine the good that could be done for fifty million dollars. The country's overrun with men needing a day's work, their families hungry, and those rattleheads are squandering a fortune to bully a broken-down nation like Spain. Why, that comes to better than six bits for each man, woman, and child in the country.

"If women only had the vote, this could never happen," she said in disgust.

"You know as well as any, Bess, that if women had the vote, there'd still be a pack of rascals up there running things," said Papa.

"It's a new age we're going into, Mrs. Wilder," Mr. Craig said. "The old order is crumbling and a new one steps in to take its place. That is the ancient tradition of mankind. Survival of the fittest. America is coming into its own. We're the greatest power on earth now, with the most advanced industries, and a strong influence for freedom."

Mama said, "That may be so, but you'd think thousands of years of suffering would have taught men the foolishness of war. There never was a good one."

The warming days of the onrushing spring brought more and more news of the outside world, which Rose devoured from the pages of the newspapers that were stacked in the kitchen. The Congress declared a war with Spain. Thousands of men volunteered to fight, lining up at recruiting offices and shouting, "We'll whip the dogs 'til they howl!"

Every boy in town had whittled a toy gun for himself out of a stick of wood, and carried it everywhere. They played war in the back-yards, and shouted slogans against the Spanish.

"We find that we want the Philippines," the newspaper writers put in their columns. "We also want Porto Rico. We may want the Carolines, the Ladrones, the Pelew, and the Mariana groups. If we do, we will take them. Much as we deplore the necessity for territorial acquisition, the people now believe the United States owes it to civilization to accept the responsibilities imposed upon it by the fortunes of war."

It excited Rose to read the stories of battle-ships steaming to far-off islands in the Pacific

Ocean, but the bloodthirsty cries for revenge scared her. She borrowed a book of maps from Mrs. Rippee and spent hours poring over the drawings of the great seas, and the tiny islands whose names she learned from reading of them.

She tried to imagine the people who lived on them, and wondered what languages they spoke. The war with Spain, all the talk and argument and the strange names, made her head spin with new ideas.

She used to think about the places the trains went, about the great cities to the east and west with their teeming streets and underground railways. Now her mind was opening even wider, like a blooming flower raising its face to the warming sunshine. Nothing had changed in her life, yet everything seemed altogether different, and unsettling.

"It's history being written, before our eyes," Paul told her one day when the Wilders went to the Cooleys' for Sunday dinner. Rose sat with him on his back stoop, throwing bits of stale corn bread to the chickens. "Gosh, it's a great time to live, don't you think?"

It was, Rose thought. She had never felt as much alive, and part of life, as she had since they moved to town. "But what if Spain wins the war? Won't it be bad for America?"

"Shucks, Rose. Nobody could beat America. We've got the muscle to lick any country now. Just let 'em try," he said, punching his hand with a fist.

Rose wished Paul wouldn't talk like the others. It made him sound like a schoolyard bully.

In May there was another great upheaval in town, when Admiral Dewey's steel cruisers sank the Spanish fleet in Manila Bay, all the way on the other side of the earth. The night the news came over the telegraph, a crowd of men and boys gathered again by the depot. They made a big pile of old barrels and set it afire.

Rose stood in the backyard, watching the big fingers of flame leaping high into the air over the roofs uptown. Her heart raced to hear the throaty cries, the crackle and roar of the flames, guns firing and drums beating. It sounded like a war. The low clouds covering the warm, humid night were lit from below with the glow of the fire. The sky looked as if it were covered in smoke, and the town was bathed in a golden haze.

Rose remembered Mama's story about hearing the ghastly drums and war cries of Indians when she lived in Indian Territory. Rose knew now just how scared Mama must have felt.

But it was also something to think about, that her own country was so strong and powerful, its reach could go halfway around the world. She couldn't help feeling a bit of pride in that.

In June the newspapers said American soldiers had landed in Cuba and were fighting the Spanish. Only a few days later, American ships captured a tiny island called Guam in the Pacific Ocean. It, too, had belonged to the Spanish.

Then, just before Independence Day, the Americans won a great battle at San Juan Hill in Cuba. The newspapers said it was a "hellish" fight, led by a new hero, Colonel

Theodore Roosevelt. But it sobered Rose to read that hundreds of American soldiers died. Hundreds of American mothers were crying that night, she thought. The children of those men would never see their fathers again.

War was not a game to be played with sticks. It was just as Mrs. Honeycutt had said, a feast for vultures.

Two days later Rose woke from a nightmare about vultures when a thundering boom shook the whole house.

"My land, that was close!" she heard Mama exclaim.

Rose's heart leaped into her throat as she tried to shake herself awake. The war had come to Mansfield! Tears welled in her eyes.

"Mama!" she cried out. "Are the Spanish coming?"

Mama let out a laugh. "No," she called out. "It's only Independence Day. They are shooting anvils off at the blacksmith's."

A moment later another shattering explosion shook her bed, and the very air pulsed with it.

Rose jumped in terror. She had heard the anvils shooting on Independence Day mornings in past years. But they had lived a mile out of town then, and the booms were far away and muffled.

Now they lived just a few houses from Murphy's blacksmith shop, where the anvils were. The explosions were deafening, and all the more frightening because there was a war on. The sound of them did not make Rose feel like celebrating. All she could think of was her nightmare.

While she dressed, shouts came from the street in front of the house. Through the open windows she could hear the words clearly, echoing off the barn. "The navy's beat 'em in Cuba. Sunk every last one of their ships. Hurrah for America!"

All that day of festivities—in the game booths, in the streets, and on the platform in the square where the mayor and other important men talked about the meaning of American freedom—people said it was a great day for the country. The Spanish had been beaten; the war was all but finished.

"However you stand on the question, that is the thing to be grateful for this day," the mayor said to the hushed crowd of picnickers on the lawn of the square. "The fightin's ended, and our Johnnies can come marching home."

"Hurrah!" the crowd roared. And the band struck up the tune "When Johnny Comes Marching Home." Everyone stood and sang their hearts out to those solemn, heavy-hearted notes. Even though Rose knew no Johnny who would come marching home to her, she felt the words deep in her breast. At the last verse she couldn't stifle a tiny sob, thinking about the Johnnies who wouldn't ever come home:

> *"Get ready for the jubilee,*
> *Hurrah! Hurrah!*
> *We'll give the heroes three times three,*
> *Hurrah! Hurrah!*
> *The laurel wreath is ready now*
> *To place upon his loyal brow,*
> *And we'll all be glad when*
> *Johnny comes marching home!"*

Cheers washed over the crowd after the last note had been played. Rose looked around and saw many shining eyes, including Mama's and even Papa's. It was a great day to be an American, to be free and to know that no nation could ever enslave Americans the way the Spanish had enslaved the peoples of those tiny islands.

The rest of that summer the newspapers told of American soldiers capturing Cuba, the city of Manila in the Philippines, Porto Rico, and Hawaii. Spain surrendered, and finally people talked less and less of war, turning their thoughts to the coming harvest season. No matter what might happen in the world, nothing was more important.

A Dirty Trick

This had been the best growing season yet, and the harvest was heavy. Abe took three full cuttings of hay off the meadows, so much that there wasn't room for it all in the barn. The rest they left stacked and capped in the pastures. They would keep it for the livestock to eat right there in the field, and what was left over they could sell when prices got high in the late winter.

The corn was tall and the ears thick with kernels. The lazy weeks of summer gave way to frantic days of cutting, shocking, and shucking. Rose spent most of her time out on

Rocky Ridge Farm, working in the fields. George Cooley came to help, and so did Effie's father, Mr. Stubbins, when he could take a little time from his own crops. Even Mr. Craig put on an old pair of Papa's overalls and helped on Saturdays.

Mama mostly stayed in town, keeping the house and working with Mrs. Cooley drying fruit, and canning tomatoes, kraut, pickles, and all the other good things they would have to eat all winter long. Now she even had a pantry in the house to store it all.

Papa was busy as ever with his draywagon, and he kept Paul working most every day.

Then came the storing of the field beans in sacks. The corn went into the crib, and some of it went to the mill to be ground into meal. The plump pumpkins were picked and stacked in the hayloft, onions were hung from the rafters of the house, white potatoes were dug and sacked, and three whole wagonloads were driven to town for sale.

The weather stayed warm and dry, and Rose loved being out on the farm again, under the clean blue sky with brightly colored butterflies and leaves tumbling in the wind. She loved working with Abe and eating meals in the little house with the babies and Nate.

As Rose, Nate, and Mr. Craig helped Abe unload the pumpkins from the wagon and stack them up in the barn, Abe told one of his stories.

"Now pumpkins is one crop you couldn't never raise on my pa's land when I was a little feist. He tried one year, but them vines growed up so big, they filled the whole hollow 'til it was level full with 'em."

Mr. Craig chuckled, and smiled broadly.

"I thought you said they couldn't grow," Rose protested, knowing as well as any of them that there was more to it than that.

"Slow down, little girl. I said he couldn't raise pumpkins," said Abe. "But them vines growed like weeds. The hollow were so danged full, it looked like a high flat field, and so thick the poor cows couldn't find the creek at the bottom.

"Pa thought he had himself a bumper crop.

But it came time to pick, and was he surprised. There weren't a pumpkin in the whole patch. The vines had growed so fast, they wore 'em out, a-dragging 'em over the rocks."

He said a neighbor of his pa's had grown a potato that was so big, it couldn't be dug from the ground. So the family built a new cabin on top of it.

"When the kids got a-hollering for something to eat, why, they just opened the trapdoor in the floor and carved out a hunk of that potato. It gave them folks good eating for fourteen years, and after that they had a fine dug basement."

Soon Mr. Craig was telling stories too, about panthers trying to come down chimneys, and about hillmen who had never seen a steamboat. When they heard its wailing whistle, they thought it was a great monster, got their guns, and went to shoot it.

Storytelling made the work go fast and filled Rose's head with wonderful pictures.

The pace of the harvest season, working from lamplight to moonlight, was withering.

Rose's hands became rough and chapped, and her body ached from bending and stooping and lifting. Meals were hasty, and every morning Mama had to call her several times to wake her from a deep, tired sleep.

But Rose enjoyed the change from town, and it made her proud to see the barn, rafters, cribs, smokehouse, pantry, and even the little space under the trapdoor in the house, all crammed with food that had been grown, nurtured, and harvested from their own land with their own hands.

One day, at the end of the harvest, Papa came to supper with a new contraption for Mama. It was a glass bottle, with metal paddles inside and a crank on top. "Now you can get rid of that old dash butter churn, Bess," he said grandly, putting the thing on the kitchen table. As he washed his hands in the basin by the door, he told them, "It's a new kind of patent butter churn. It'll bring the butter in three minutes, guaranteed."

Rose and Mama peered at the glass jar. "It looks complicated," said Mama. "All this machinery. I don't know why I have to give up my dash. It has served us well all these years."

In the corner sat the dash, a tall earthen crock with an earthen lid that had a hole in it. The dasher was a wooden stick with blocks of wood nailed on one end. Mama and Rose always took turns plunging the dasher up and down, and it took a lot of effort and time to make the butter come.

"Simplest thing in the world," Papa declared, wiping his hands dry on the roller towel. "Look here. You just pull out the beaters and the crank, pour the cream in, put the beaters back and turn the crank. Why, there's hardly a chore in the world some fellow hasn't figured a way to make short work of it."

Papa took the old churn and stored it in the barn.

The next day Mama used the patent churn. She tried holding the glass in her hand as she cranked, but it was too big and clumsy to hold and crank at the same time. Rose tried, but she could hardly turn the crank at all. Mama set it on the table, but the cranking made it jump around clumsily. Finally she set it on the floor and put her foot on top while she cranked.

The butter did come quickly, but Mama said her back ached when she was done, and when she went to clean it, she couldn't unscrew the paddles from the shaft. The sharp edges of the metal parts cut her fingers.

That night she complained to Papa. "It was very thoughtful of you, Manly. But I just can't get the hang of it. I wish you'd bring in my old churn."

"Probably just takes a bit of experience," he said, looking at the parts of it. "You can churn in three minutes with this, and the old one takes half a day. Put one end of a board on the churn and the other on a chair. Then you can sit on the board and crank with both hands."

The next time Mama wanted to churn, she did just that, sitting on a board as if she were horseback riding. The churn bucked some, but Mama managed to hold her seat. Then she cut herself again, trying to take it apart to wash.

"I'll tell you a secret," she told Rose. "I hate this thing. I don't know what it is about your father sometimes. He gets an idea in his head and can't see what's right in front of his face. Men can be so mule-headed."

She complained again to Papa. "Manly, I really do wish you'd bring in the old churn. I cut myself again trying to clean that new one."

"Oh, pshaw," Papa said with a wave of his hand. "Think of the time you're saving. You're just being old-fashioned, is all. This thing brings the butter in three minutes."

Mama sighed and said no more. She kept on fighting the patent churn, and the churn kept fighting her back. She didn't want to hurt Papa's feelings, so she kept her complaints to herself.

The winter term of school began, and Rose was shocked to find that Blanche and Lois had moved up to the Fifth Reader, in Professor Bland's classroom across the hall from Mrs. Honeycutt. That was a terribly lonely first day, although she still had the Hibbard twins to talk to and they took turns sitting with her.

The only good thing Rose could think of was

that Paul had moved up too, to the Sixth Reader. At least he and Lois wouldn't be in the same classroom.

All summer and fall Paul had been walking Lois home from church. Every Sunday Rose had to hide her ache, and pretend to listen with interest when Paul talked about what a nice girl she was, and how her father was foursquare and solid.

Rose hadn't seen much of Blanche since the last school session ended. Rose had been very busy with chores and farmwork, and Blanche's father had taken her family for a trip that summer to Chicago.

At recess on the first day of school, Lois bragged to the other girls about Paul walking her home. "He's my first beau," she said haughtily, jingling her bracelet. "And I think he's terribly sweet. It's plain he likes *me* well enough."

Rose clenched her teeth in silence.

"D'you think he'll ask you to marry?" breathed Blanche.

"Oh, I wouldn't know about that," Lois said

breezily. "I'm only fourteen, and mother says that's too young to even think about such things. Besides, there are so many fish in the sea. How could a girl know if she caught just the right one?"

The Hibbard twins and Blanche thought that was terribly funny and giggled crazily, but Rose's heart was hard as a stone. She still couldn't understand how Paul could like such a girl.

The next week there was a pie supper one night at school. Rose helped Mama bake an apple pie. Outside the window, a thin layer of snow lay on the yard. Sunshine struck across the geraniums in their painted tins on the windowsill.

The table was perfectly neat, just the way Mama liked everything when she cooked. The rolling pin and sifter, the bowl of peeled apples and the cinnamon, nutmeg, butter, and brown sugar were all lined up in a row. Papa preferred brown sugar and a dash of nutmeg in his pie.

Rose had never been to a pie supper, and she wanted to know what it was.

"It's an auction, to raise money for books and school things," Mama explained as she mixed the dough for the crust. "The young ladies and women all donate pies or cakes, and wrap each one nicely in paper and ribbons, so no one can know what is inside or who made it. The men all bid on them, and when one man wins the high bid, he sits and eats it with the girl who baked it."

Mama laid the crust in the pan, and Rose carefully cut the extra off with a knife and crimped the dough around the edge.

"But if the men don't know who made them, how will Papa know this pie's for him?"

"Papa will know this is my pie, because I'll let him see the wrapping. It wouldn't be proper for a married woman to eat her pie or cake with another man. But a young lady will be very careful not to let on which is hers, unless of course she wants her beau to know about it."

A pie supper sounded like fun, and Rose couldn't wait to see it.

The next night Rose walked with Mama and Papa up the street in the wintry darkness to school, along with clutches of other people. The young ladies had their baked goods hidden under old quilts and blankets, or wrapped in newspaper, so no one would see how they were decorated.

The married women, like Mama, carried theirs right out in plain sight. Mama had wrapped hers in white crepe paper, and tied it with a red ribbon.

The hard-packed earth of the school yard was littered with buggies and wagons. Inside the school was full of milling grown-ups. Rose always thought the schoolhouse looked so strange, like a different place, when it was full of grown-ups.

The auction would take place in Professor Kay's Third Reader classroom. Professor Kay was a auctioneer when he wasn't teaching, so naturally he would be in charge of the bidding.

All the men waited in another classroom while the girls and women took their baked goods into Professor Kay's room. No man or boy was supposed to peek, but Rose heard some of the young men bragging that their sweethearts had told them which one to bid on.

"You keep your mouths shut when they put up the pasteboard box with the yellow fringe and the pink ribbon," one of them shouted above the noisy voices. "That's my Emily's banana cream pie, and ain't nobody going to eat it with her but me."

"We'll just see about it," another joked. "The high bid takes the cake. Hope you brought a fistful of money, sonny."

Two long tables at the front of Professor Kay's room quickly piled up with beautifully wrapped cakes and pies. Some were in boxes that were covered with colorful scraps of fabric. Others were wrapped in paper, and two or three had only old newspaper over them. Each one was a mystery that would soon be revealed.

The most beautiful of them all had a whole bouquet of silk flowers on top. Lois had brought it and carefully set it in front of all the others.

Rose was looking at everything, when suddenly a pair of hands covered her eyes from behind. She whirled around. It was Paul. His hair was damp and neatly combed. He smelled of bay rum, and his face was freshly scrubbed. His deep, dark eyes sparkled marvelously.

"Hey, Rose. Is one of them yours?"

"No," said Rose, wishing one were so she could tell Paul. Maybe he'd buy it and eat it with her.

"I'll tell you a secret," he whispered. "That one over there, the one with the green paper and the big yellow bow? That's Lois'. She told me, and I'm going to buy it."

Rose had seen Lois come in and put down her donation. But it wasn't that one at all. It was the prettiest one, with the bouquet on it.

"But Paul," she started to say.

Just then Professor Kay's voice boomed out. The auction was starting. Paul hurried to the back, where all the men and boys were standing about nervously, poking each other, whispering, and grinning.

Rose sat down with Mama in one of the chairs that had been brought in to replace the low school desks. She was confused; there must be some mistake.

"Mama, Paul thinks Lois' baking is the one . . ." she started to say. But Mama shushed her to be still.

"What we have here, gentlemen, is a sampling of the cream and butter of the local crop," Professor Kay began, sweeping his arm toward the groaning tables. "Let me tell you good folks that I have done a scientific calculation of the labor it took to turn out these fine examples of gustatory enticement."

The crowd laughed.

"By my reckoning—and I am a man to be reckoned with—some two hundred hours of beating, folding, mixing, and kneading went into all this. And enough sugar, honey, and molasses to choke a spring bear.

"So I hope you boys came with bulging pockets and hearts filled with respect for the womenfolk in our little village. We're aiming for top dollar on every item. Any nickel-nursers among you are going to go hungry tonight!"

The crowd laughed again, and the auction began. Professor Kay held the packages up, one by one, and talked so fast Rose could hardly understand but a word or two.

Her eyes shot from Professor Kay to the back, where the boys and men stood. Those who didn't bid folded their arms across their chests. Those who did raised their hands to signal the price they would pay.

"I'm-sellin'-cakes'n'pies-cakes'n'pies-cakes'n'pies-ain't-nobody-gonna-stop-me-from-sellin'-cakes'n'pies-what-am-I-bid-on-this-beautiful-blue-box-five-cent-five-cent-five-five-ten-ten-cent-ten-and-I-have-fifteen-twenty-twenty-five-eeny-meeny-miny-mo-what's-the-price-it's-gonna-go?-thirty-thirty-gimme-thirty-thirty-five-step-in-step-out-make-your-bid-before-I-shout-SOLD! to the young hayseed over by the window," he said, pointing. "Your mama know you ain't tucked in your bed, sonny?"

The crowd roared as a young country man, blushing fiercely, ambled forward and took the package. His sweetheart got up and followed him to the back, giggling helplessly, her face as red as his.

The auction was more fun than Rose had ever known. Professor Kay made good-natured jokes on everyone, and some of the men bid fiercely for some of the packages.

Finally Mama's apple pie came up, and nobody bid against Papa. He bought the pie for fifty cents.

"Why didn't anyone else bid?" Rose asked Mama.

"Because everyone knows when a married man bids, he's bidding for his wife's package. It wouldn't be right for another man to bid against him."

Two more cakes went, and then it was the green package with the yellow bow that Paul said was Lois'. Rose held her breath.

Paul bid twenty-five cents right off the bat.

"Whoa, now," Professor Kay boomed. "Here's an eager beaver. I reckon this whippersnapper thinks he's got the inside track. You fellas gonna let him get away with it? thirty-thirty-thirty-do-I-hear-forty-forty-has-it-up-and-coming-beat-the-price-or-just-get-going . . ."

Poor Paul had given himself away with his

eagerness. Some other boys were playing a trick on him, bidding against him, forcing him to pay more and more for that package.

Paul's face grew furrowed, and his eyes darkened with anger. Those boys pushed his bid higher and higher—seventy-five cents, eighty cents. The price just kept going up, and the crowd was whooping and hollering.

Then, all of a sudden, no one else was bidding. "Dollar-fifty-fifty-fifty-dollar-and-four-bits-going-going-*SOLD*!" Professor Kay thundered. "To the new poor boy in town."

Paul grinned with relief, shot a glance at Lois, and began to walk forward to collect his package.

Then Mrs. Rippee stood up.

Rose gasped. Horrible, wicked guffaws broke out among the men.

Paul stopped dead in his tracks, a stricken look in his eyes. He stared at Lois, who turned away with a sly, guilty look.

"My, my," Mrs. Rippee exclaimed with a big smile. "And I thought my time was past."

A ripple of nervous laughter ran through the crowd.

"Well, now, here's a boy who's really got respect for his elders," Professor Kay joked.

Rose wasn't laughing; she could have cried to see the look on Paul's face. Lois had pulled a dirty, low-down trick on him. Now he was the laughingstock of the whole pie supper.

The rest of the evening was ruined for Rose. She wanted to sit with Paul and Mrs. Rippee, and share the upside-down pineapple cake Mrs. Rippee had made, but she couldn't gather up the courage. Rose glared at Lois, whose pie was won by an older boy in the Sixth Reader. She sat with him, giggling and jingling her bracelet.

Mama broke away from a group of Eastern Star ladies she was talking to and came to where Rose was sitting with Papa and Nate. Nate had bid a nickel on just about every package, but he hadn't won a single one, so he helped Papa polish off Mama's pie.

Mama leaned over and whispered in her ear, "What did I tell you about Lois and Paul? Time always tells the truth."

"I remember," said Rose. "I feel terrible. Poor Paul."

"It'll just take him some time to earn that money back. And he'll live down the shame, too," said Mama. "Go over and sit with them. I'm sure there's enough for you to have a piece. And Paul might use a friendly face about now."

Paul sat stone-faced while Mrs. Rippee chattered about a pie supper she had gone to as a young girl.

"I was just telling Paul here about some of the jokes folks used to play on each other," Mrs. Rippee said, smiling warmly at Paul. She patted his knee. "I know it wasn't my company you were after, young man. Don't take it too much to heart. Any girl who'd be so scheming and deceitful wouldn't make much of a sweetheart anyway."

Paul's lips stayed clamped shut and he looked at Rose pitifully. He stabbed absentmindedly at his cake and stole little glances at Lois. Rose knew just how he felt; he wanted to run from the room. But he must be polite to Mrs. Rippee and stay.

Rose couldn't think of a thing worth saying.

She hated seeing him all twisted with anger and hurt, like a whipped dog, but she was delighted that Paul would not be walking Lois home from church anymore.

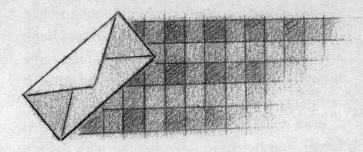

End of an Era

One morning the patent churn cut Mama's hand badly. Rose was sweeping the dining room when it happened. Mama cried out in pain and frustration.

"Oh, this blasted thing!"

Rose watched in shock as Mama grabbed the contraption, opened the kitchen door, and threw it hard as she could out into the yard. Through the window Rose could see it land on its handle with a crash, and then bounce.

Next Mama marched outside and gave it a furious kick. Rose had to stifle a giggle. She'd never seen Mama so riled up.

Then Mama picked it up and looked at it. The handle was broken off, the shaft was bent, and the beater paddles were a wreck. She brought it back into the kitchen and hid it behind the little curtain under the washstand.

Rose was speechless. Mama took a deep breath and began to wrap her cut with a scrap of old cloth.

Rose tiptoed to the kitchen door. "Are you all right?" she asked meekly.

"I feel just on top of the world," Mama sang out in a defiant voice. "And that's all I care to say on the matter." Then she went on about her chores as if nothing had happened. She even whistled as she worked. Rose was befuddled, but she didn't dare mention that churn.

As soon as Papa came in for dinner, Rose watched Mama like a hawk. She was brisk and efficient as always getting the meal on the table, but just before the men came to sit down, she cornered Papa in the kitchen.

"I want you to bring in that old churn. I've cream that needs dashing."

"But Bess," Papa said, "you can churn in just

three minutes with the new one. What's the use to spend half a day . . . ?"

"I can't," Mama declared. "It's broken."

"Why, how did it happen?" asked Papa.

"I dropped it," she admitted. Then she added in a small voice, "Just as far as I could." She fetched the mangled churn and handed it to him. Papa turned it over in his hands and looked at Mama in wonderment. He slowly shook his head.

"Gee whillikins, Bess. I wish you'd told me you didn't like to churn with it. I could have used the wheels and shaft for something else, but now they're ruined."

Mama just sighed. "You'd best go and sit down. I've got a hot meal to serve."

Papa looked at Rose as he passed out of the kitchen, rolled his eyes, and shrugged. Mama was right. Men could be terribly mule-headed.

That winter brought tragic news from Papa's family. In a letter from his sister Eliza Jane in Louisiana, Papa read that Grandpa Wilder had lost his fortune.

Grandpa had given his money to Eliza Jane

and to Papa's brother Perley. They had put nearly all of it into rice farms. Something had gone wrong. Rose didn't understand what, but something terrible had happened, and now the money was gone.

Papa was very sober after the letter came. He sat for a long time in the parlor after supper, long after his usual time to go to bed. Rose lay awake in her own bed, listening for his footsteps, wanting him to come to bed. It worried her to think of him just sitting there in the easy chair with that letter in his hand.

Almost nothing ever had pulled down Papa's spirits, except the death of Mr. Cooley. Grandpa losing his money must be like a death, Rose thought.

Mama got up twice to check on Papa. Rose could hear their soft muffled voices coming up through the parlor ceiling into the attic. Finally Papa came to bed, and Rose could let herself drift off to sleep.

The next morning was Saturday. Papa was out working, and Mama had gone to Reynolds'. Rose was tidying up when she found Aunt Eliza Jane's letter on the windowsill by Papa's side of the bed. She knew she shouldn't read it, but her curiosity was too strong to resist. She sat on the edge of the bed and learned the terrible facts:

Dearest Manzo,

I have not sat down to write you these past months as I was too distraught and could not think how to describe to you the terrible situation in which we find ourselves. You know, of course, that Father gave Perley and me the chance to put his estate to good use.

As this is principally rice country, we thought it prudent to use Father's money to buy some useful ground that would bring an increase both from the sale of crops and improvement of the land. We found the land, a fertile sixty acres bordering a bayou, which is a kind of ever-flowing swampy river common to this country.

Rice takes a layer of water over it for a good part of the season, and during the infrequent dry spells the bayou would supply it, so

*long as we could find a way to pump it up
onto the fields. The land needed preparation,
but we had counted on the good supply of
cheap labor to work it for us.*

*The man who sold us the property was well
known here in Crowley, and he seemed to be
an honest and respectable businessman. You
can imagine how thunderstruck we were to
find that the deed carried a substantial
hidden lien on it, some thousands of dollars
plus interest, that had to be paid off before we
could legally take possession.*

*But there was not near enough money left
to do this, and the lienholder would not
relent.*

*To make matters worse, the man who sold
it to us has disappeared, along with Father's
hard-earned estate. The authorities have
issued a warrant for his arrest for commit-
ting a fraud. But we have been advised to
keep little hope that we will ever see a cent.*

*Manzo, we are all devastated by this turn
of bad luck. Father's whole life, the careful
building up of his farms, his devotion to*

*thrift and industry, has been stolen away by
the stroke of a pen. I am afraid for Father's
health, as well. He has taken the news poorly.
For a week he would not rise from his bed,
and still speaks only when he must.*

*We children, Perley and I, will survive as we
always have. We are not so old that we cannot
make a new start. And anyone such as those of
us who have risen from the ashes of the unfor-
giving prairie can certainly come back and
thrive in this prosperous and fertile region.*

*But Father is old and has no heart to fight.
Mother dear is at her wits' end with worry
for him.*

*I am so sorry to be the bearer of such
unhappy tidings. I wish you were here, to
lend a little of your quiet strength and love.
God bless and keep you and Laura, with special kisses for my favorite niece, dearest Rose.*

With eternal devotion, your loving sister,

Eliza Jane

Rose folded the letter and carefully put it
back on the sill exactly the way she had found

it. She thought hard as she swept the floors. She didn't understand some of the things Eliza wrote about, liens and fraud and such.

She did understand the calamity that had befallen Grandpa. He had been rich, and in an instant he had lost it all, his life's work vanished without a trace.

Although her relatives in Louisiana were far away and not so well known to Rose, she understood why Papa was so disturbed. She remembered that when Grandpa and Grandma Wilder had visited two summers back, Papa had tried to talk Grandpa into staying in Missouri.

Grandpa had said the Ozark hills were too stony and steep for good farming. He had heard that there were opportunities to increase his money in Louisiana. Then, just before they left on the train, Grandpa bought the house they now lived in from Mrs. Cooley and gave it to Mama and Papa.

Rose would always remember Grandpa's words as he explained himself to Papa: "I'm an old man and I won't walk this earth forever.

Consider it part of my bequest to you, son."

One night that following spring, a delivery boy from the depot interrupted their dinner with a telegram. Without reading it, Papa said straightaway, "It's Father."

Papa gave the boy a nickel and handed the telegram to Mama. She opened it, read for a moment, and just nodded her head. Papa sighed heavily. Grandpa Wilder was dead.

"I need a bit of peace and quiet," he said softly. "Think I'll saddle up May and go for a ride out in the country."

"Of course," Mama said. Then she hugged him.

When he had gone, and the dishes were washed and the floors swept clean, Rose asked Mama, "Will Papa go to Louisiana?"

"I think not," said Mama. "It's planting season. There's too much work to be done here, and Papa could never get all the way down there in time to help bury him."

"It's terribly sad, isn't it?"

"More than you can know, Rose," Mama

said. "It is the end of an era. My folks and your father's folks, they were the first to settle this part of the country. It nearly killed them, and they had no help from anyone except their neighbors and the grace of God, which was in scarce supply. Every destructive element was thrown in their path, but they survived by hard work, faith, and family devotion.

"Now the frontier is closed, and the old folks are starting to go to their rewards. The country will never see the likes of them again. They are the true American heroes, not tin soldiers like Colonel Roosevelt.

"That is why I like to tell you stories from the old days. You must remember them, Rose. They are your history, and the history of this country. One day, when you have children of your own, you will want to pass them along."

"Yes, Mama," Rose said solemnly. "I promise with all my heart."

Mama got up from her chair, put her hands on her hips, and arched her back to get out the kinks.

"Now let us get on with living," she said.

"We can at least be grateful we didn't follow your father's family to Louisiana, and lose our shirts along with them."

Papa stayed quiet for weeks and weeks after that. He never was one to cry. Rose never had seen him do it, and she would have been surprised if he had. He carried his grief around inside him, like a heavy weight dragging him down.

Rose felt so helpless watching him eat his dinner without pleasure, eyes downcast and no glimmer of humor crinkling the corners of his eyes, or making his mustache quiver the way it did when he told or heard a joke.

Rose pondered how hard it was to live a life without finding some sorrow in it. She was only twelve years old, but she thought she had found enough sorrow already to last a lifetime.

The Tramp

On one of the first summery days of spring, Nate was helping Rose hoe the garden behind the house in town when Mama called them in.

"I'm almost out of flour, and all the baking yet to be done. I don't have time to dress up and go get more," she said. "Why don't you two run uptown and fetch me ten pounds? Here's a nickel to buy yourselves a sack of candy."

"Gosh, thanks, Mrs. Wilder," Nate said excitedly. Rose was delighted, too. Mama had just started letting Rose go uptown by herself, and doing errands on her own made her feel important.

The two children watched the morning local pass by heading east. Then they climbed the stony grade to walk the short distance down the tracks into town. That was Nate's idea. He said sometimes the boys found pennies along the tracks, and one time a boy found a perfectly good pocketknife.

Behind them the train rumbled away. They heard the screech of its brakes and turned to see the fireman throw a shovelful of coal down the embankment far down the tracks. Then the train chuffed hard as it picked up speed again.

"Why do they do that?" Rose wondered. "I've seen them do it before. Why would they throw away perfectly good coal?"

"Dunno," Nate said. "Let's go look."

So they walked the opposite direction, away from town. As they got close to the place where the fireman had thrown down the coal, they heard a rustling in the thick bushes down at the bottom of the embankment.

They stopped. Nate crouched down and pulled Rose down beside him.

"What do you think it is?" Rose whispered.

"Sounds like some varmint," said Nate.

They crept forward until finally they could see right down where the noise was coming from. A man was stooped over, gathering up the chunks of coal and tossing them into a dirty old sack.

The man was tall and thin. He had no hat to cover his red hair. His overalls were wrinkled, and rags bound up his shoes. He was so busy, he hadn't seen them, but then Rose accidentally kicked a pebble against one of the rails. It *ping*ed, and the man's head snapped up.

His hand stopped in midair with a piece of coal in it, and his eyes glared at them stony and tense, like the eyes of a startled animal thinking whether to fight or run. Nate flinched. Rose's heart skipped a beat. She thought he might throw the coal at them.

But then his face relaxed, he smiled, and he went back to picking up the coal, as if they weren't even there.

"Howdy, mister," Nate said. "Whatcha doin'?"

"What's it look like?" the man said without looking up. Rose was surprised to hear such a smooth young voice coming from his soot-grimed face.

"It looks like you're stealing coal from the railroad," Nate said. Rose jabbed him in the ribs for being rude.

"Hey!" Nate complained.

"You might say that," the man said, stopping and resting a hand on his knee. "You might say that if the railroad men didn't throw it down here for me to pick up."

"Why?" Rose piped up. "Why would they throw away coal?"

"They don't throw it away, young lady. They put it here for fellows like me to find, out of kindness. You see, I'm a tramp. Well, I'm a schoolteacher, or used to be. But right now I'm a tramp, and this coal here keeps me nice and warm of a cool spring evening."

Rose was fascinated. Tramps often came to the kitchen door looking for a few hours' work and something to eat. Mama had no work, and anyway she wouldn't like to hire a tramp, but she would always give them a hunk of bread, or a cold boiled potato.

When they talked, those tramps hardly ever looked at you square, and when they did, their eyes were often mean and icy, or hangdog. They spoke poorly, and only when they must.

The red-haired man looked squarely at Rose and Nate with gentle blue eyes and scratched his red beard. He spoke as properly as Mama and Papa.

"Where's your house?" Rose asked. "Do you live in town?"

The tramp shook his head and chuckled as if he'd heard a good joke. He bent over and went back to gathering the coal. "You're looking at my little mansion right now," he said. "Just a hollow place in the ground with some brush overhead to keep off the rain. A tramp doesn't have a house. That's what makes him a tramp; he's a fellow down on his luck, sleeping where night catches him, and living on day work and handouts."

He picked up the last bit of coal, even the

broken scraps, hefted the sack onto his shoulder, and turned to go, like a rumpled, skinny Santa Claus. Then he stopped and called over his shoulder, "Say, you kids hear of any work around, you give a shout."

"My papa says this is a boom town," Rose said helpfully. "They're even building a new railroad to Ava. You could help build the railroad."

"Railroad's got its own men," he said. "And most folks don't like to hire a tramp. Anyway, who'd have me, looking the way I do?" He laughed at himself, but Rose couldn't see the joke in it. She felt sorry for him. She wanted to do something.

"How could we find you?" she asked.

"Right here, for now. My sleeping spot's just over yonder. But tomorrow, you never can tell." Then he loped off into the brush.

Rose and Nate hurried into town to fetch the flour before Mama would need it and scold them for dawdling. While the clerk went to the back to get the sack, Nate eyed the candy jars with greedy eyes.

"Let's get some of this tutti-frutti gum,

Rose. And some gumdrops, and stick candy."

Rose looked at all those colorful jars but she couldn't think about candy. She looked around the store, at the fat, creamy wheel of cheese, the barrels of crackers and pickles, boxes of salt pork, and tins of sardines. The men who lounged around the store were always snacking on sardines and crackers. Rose hated sardines, but the men seemed to like them.

"Here's your flour," the clerk said as he dropped the sack on top of a barrel. A little puff of wheat dust shot into the air.

"We want a nickel's worth of candy, sir," Nate said. "First we want some tutti-frutti gum. Two pieces. Then . . ."

"We don't want any candy," Rose said matter-of-factly.

"Hey, Rose! What's the idea? Your mama gave us a nickel for it. You got the nickel right there in your hand."

"We don't want any candy," Rose repeated sternly. "We want a nickel's worth of sardines and crackers."

"Sardines and crackers! I hate sardines!"

Nate wailed. "I want candy."

"Please, sir," Rose said, handing the clerk her coin. "A nickel's worth of sardines and crackers. Wrapped in paper."

The clerk shrugged and went to get it.

"What're you up to, anyway?" Nate groused. "I'm not eating any of that. You're cheatin' me out of my rightful candy."

"We're not going to buy candy, because we're going to buy something good to eat for that tramp," said Rose. "And I won't hear a word against it."

"But . . . but," Nate sputtered. "That's just plain dumb, Rose. Who cares about an old tramp? It's our nickel. We can spend it like we want."

Rose jammed her fists onto her hips and stared Nate in the eye. "Listen to me. Don't talk like a selfish brat. We can get candy 'most anytime we like. But that poor man has to beg for his food. Didn't you see how thin he was? We're going to take him something to eat, and that's all."

"Aw, Rose," Nate whined. "Shucks, I had

my mouth all watered up for candy. Shucks."
He looked mournfully at the jars brimming
with colorful sweets, and his fingers caressed
the lids.

"Shame on you, Nate Baird. You ought to
know better'n anybody how awful it is to go
hungry."

Nate quickly turned his face away and
scuffed the toe of his shoe against the floor.
Rose had embarrassed him with the memory of
his trying to steal eggs from Mama's henhouse
all those years ago, when he was a little hungry
boy dressed in rags. Rose knew he wouldn't
give her any more trouble now.

They hurried down the tracks to the place
where they had met the tramp.

"Hello!" Rose called out. "Mister, are you
out there?"

But the only answer was the sighing of the
wind in the wires, and the raucous cawing of
crows. They clambered down the embankment and looked around the bushes, but they
couldn't find his sleeping place. So they left
the package of sardines and crackers on top of

an old stump right by the embankment, where he would be sure to see it.

"I bet that was a waste of a good nickel," Nate said. "Some animal's going to get it."

"I don't care," said Rose. "At least we tried to do him a good turn."

When they got back to the house with the flour, Mama stood at the kitchen door, her hands coated with flour. She was cross.

"Land sakes, Rose. I've been waiting to finish this ball of dough, and you off gadding about town. What took you so long?"

"I'm sorry, Mama. We saw a tramp along the tracks, and then we got him some sardines and crackers with our nickel. He looked real hungry. But he wasn't there when we went back, so we left it on a stump. Maybe Papa knows of work for him."

"He'll never find that food," Nate chimed in. "Some animal's going to get it for sure."

Mama stared at them as if they had lost their senses. "What tramp? What stump? What animal?"

Rose explained herself, more slowly this

time, while Mama floured the ball of dough and kneaded it.

When Rose was done, Mama said she admired her generous spirit. "But I don't like you children fooling around with tramps. Some of them are rough characters, and I have heard they can carry smallpox. I want you to stay away from those tracks, and any tramps, you hear?"

"Yes'm," they both answered.

But even as she said it, Rose was making other plans. That man was not a rough character; anyone could see it. The next morning at breakfast, when Mama was in the dining room serving the meal, Rose slipped a few biscuits into her apron pocket, along with a piece of sausage she wrapped in a bit of old newspaper.

She sneaked the food out of the house when she went to walk Bunting to pasture. On her way back, she dashed down an alley next to the Robinetts' house that ran right up to the tracks. She found the spot where the coal had been thrown.

The tramp wasn't there, but she spied a bit

of smoke curling from behind a hickory tree nearby. She made her way through the brush and found him on the other side of the tree, sitting in front of a little fire of wood and coal.

He jumped up at first when he saw her. Then he folded his tall, lean body and squatted down again on his heels.

"Hello," Rose said.

"Hello there," the tramp said, stirring the fire with a stick. "You surprised me. I don't get much in the way of visitors, unless it's some farmer or lawman come to chase me off."

Rose felt tongue-tied all of a sudden. She took out the biscuits and the wrapped sausage and held it out to him.

"What's this?" he said, his flaming eyebrows arching curiously.

"It's just some food, from our breakfast. We had too much and . . . I hated to give it to the chickens," she lied.

"Is that so?" the tramp said. "Well, I reckon I ought to be able to eat as well as any chicken. I thank you kindly." He smiled and reached out to take the food from Rose's hand. She was surprised to see that his hands were pink and clean. Then she noticed that his face was shaved, too.

"You the one that left the sardines?"

"Yes!" Rose said excitedly. "You found them."

"I did, and I thank you twice. You're quite a nice young lady, to be so kind to a fellow like me. But I don't think your mother and father will like it much if they find out you've been stealing food. Folks don't like tramps much. It could turn out badly for both of us."

Rose blushed. "I didn't steal the sardines," she said softly. "I bought them with my candy money. But how did you know about the biscuits and sausage?"

"I think you better go now," the man said abruptly, standing up. His lips wobbled an instant, and his eyes grew mournful. Then, just as quickly, his face hardened. "By rights you shouldn't be here. Go on home now, and leave me be. Go on."

He turned and walked away into the brush, leaving Rose stunned and confused. She watched him go and then made her way back to the tracks, and down the grade to the house.

All day she thought about the tramp, and when she went to bed and heard the patter of rain on the roof over her head, she worried whether he was dry and warm.

The next morning, she snitched more biscuits, and a piece of salt pork. She went again to the tramp's sleeping place. Again he was startled to see her.

"I thought I told you to stay away from here," he said. His voice was stern, but she could see in his eyes that he was glad to see her.

"I was worried," said Rose. "It rained last night, and I was worried you got wet."

"It's not so bad," he said, shrugging. "I've been in worse spots, when I was in Cuba."

"You were in Cuba?" Rose said in astonishment. "You fought the Spanish in Cuba?"

The tramp laughed wickedly. "You could call it that," he said. "Mostly we were fighting the mosquitoes and the mud and the rotten meat they sent us. If folks only knew . . ." Then he stopped and sighed. "Well, just forget about all that. Here you are, trying to help out a poor fool like me, and I'm kicking about it. My name's Jim. What's yours?"

Rose squatted down by the fire and talked with Jim. He said he came from Kansas. He was a teacher, and then he volunteered to fight the Spanish. But after he came home from the war, he couldn't find work. "I just haven't had a day's worth of luck since," he said. "That's the spoils of war, I reckon."

Just then an express thundered past, spewing a rolling cloud of smoke over everything. Rose realized she was late getting home. She hurriedly said good-bye. "I'll come again," she promised.

"You do that, Rose," said Jim. "And I thank you with all my heart for the grub. Your ma makes the best biscuits I ever ate, but I don't think you ought to be stealing food. I get by all right. Don't you worry about me."

Rose went back every day for the next week. It was hard to sneak away sometimes, and Mama almost caught her one day filching a piece of corn bread. She never stayed long, for fear Mama would miss her. And Jim didn't say much anyway. He always seemed glad to see her, but anxious for her to go, too.

Then, one day after dinner when Mama was washing dishes and Rose was clearing the table in the dining room, her heart leaped into her throat when she overheard Mama say, "Manly, I think we need to start locking the doors. I've been missing food."

"It's springtime," Papa said absentmindedly, rattling his newspaper. "We always eat better when we start working hard in the fields."

"No, it's not that," said Mama. "I know I had eight potatoes in that bowl last night, and now there are only six. And we've been going through an awful lot of biscuits and corn bread. I think someone's been sneaking in when we aren't around and helping themselves. I wouldn't be surprised if it was that tramp Rose saw down the tracks."

"That's bad news," said Papa, turning the page. "I hate to cause extra trouble for a fellow that's hit a rough patch, but I reckon I better see the sheriff this afternoon. He'll roust the man and send him on his way. We don't want a thief lurking about town."

Rose was horrified. She was caught in a trap, and as she soberly went about her work, her mind struggled to find a way to escape. She must warn Jim, but if she did, he would go away and she couldn't help him anymore. If she did nothing, the sheriff would run him out of town, or maybe even put him in jail.

Papa drained the last of the coffee from his cup, folded up the paper, and pushed his chair back. "I've got a load to pick up at the depot," he said. "I'll stop and see Sheriff Lockwood about that tramp."

Rose stood there with her hands full of dirty dishes, paralyzed, her heart beating thickly. Papa pulled on his coat and started toward the front door. Rose's mind skipped over her choices.

Papa took his hat off the hall tree, brushed the brim with his cuff, and set in on his head. He reached out to turn the door handle.

"Papa, wait!" Rose shouted. "Don't go. I . . . The tramp. I mean . . . Don't tell the sheriff. It wasn't him. It wasn't the tramp who took the food."

Papa's eyebrows pinched inquisitively. Rose heard Mama's footsteps coming out of the kitchen.

"What do you mean?" Mama asked, wiping her hands on her apron. "What do you know about it?"

Rose heaved a sigh of dread and set the dirty dishes down on the table. Then she confessed everything. Papa took off his hat and coat and sat back down at the table. He stroked his mustache and pulled at his chin.

They listened to Rose without a peep, although Mama shifted her weight now and then.

Rose didn't cry. She was much too old for that. Besides, she felt miserable enough without tears. She was sorry, more sorry than she'd ever been. She had disobeyed Mama. She had deceived her and Papa. And she was a thief.

"I couldn't bear the thought of him going hungry," Rose pleaded. "I just had to do something, and I thought you wouldn't approve."

"Well, I'll be starched," Papa said. "Doesn't that beat all?"

"Are you about finished?" Mama asked gravely. Rose nodded. "I don't know which thing you have told us is worst: that you lied, that you disobeyed me, that you—"

"Now hold your horses, Bess," Papa butted in. "Just calm yourself and think about it. Rose has apologized. She knows she did wrong. But I say she's done a brave thing, too. She saved that fellow from getting run out of town, or locked up. A poor soldier boy who's probably seen some terrible things and hardly knows which way to turn."

"Well, I . . . But Manly, Rose must learn that there are dangers. You don't want her adopting every loafer and scoundrel that wanders into town."

Rose could hardly believe her ears. Mama and Papa were arguing, right in front of her.

"You really think we raised a girl that foolish?" Papa asked sternly.

"Well, no. Of course not," Mama said, wringing her hands. "But . . ."

"No buts about it," said Papa firmly. "I'm not saying we ought to give Rose a parade. But let's look at it reasonable like. She tried to do a good deed. Her heart was in the right place. We taught her that much.

"And you know as well as I that if she'd come straight out and asked if we could help this Jim fellow, we'd probably have done it."

"Yes, I suppose. Well, of course," said Mama, the lines in her face smoothing. She looked at Rose with tenderness softening her eyes. "I am proud of you for owning up to your mistake, Rose, but I just can't help worrying about you. A mother always does. You're . . . you're everything to us, Papa and me."

Rose felt her heart melting. A lump in her throat kept her from saying that she worried about Mama and Papa, too, and that they were everything to her.

"It's just that you're strongheaded and willful sometimes," Mama said. "I'd just hate it if anything should happen because you lost your head over some foolish notion."

"I'm sorry, Mama," Rose said. "I'm sorry to

worry you. I'll try not to be so willful."

"Well, all right then. And I'm sorry to be so hard on you. Let's just put it behind us."

"Sounds like a fine idea," Papa said, pushing back his chair and standing. "Now, Rose, let's you and I go see about this Jim. I'm nobody in this town if I can't find a willing, able-bodied man some work and a proper meal."

Best of Friends

Poor Jim's eyes flew wide with terror when he saw Rose coming through the brush with Papa. He started to run, until Papa called out, "Hold up there, Jim! I'm no lawman."

It took a few moments to convince him that Papa had come to help, not to chase him away. Papa insisted that he come back to the house, where he could bathe and have a good wholesome meal. At first Jim wouldn't go.

"I'm mighty poor company, Mr. Wilder," he said. "Ever since Cuba, I just don't feel fit to be around folks."

But Papa pressed him, in quiet tones, the way he would gentle a balky horse. Finally Jim gave in. As they walked home, some of the neighbors gawked. Jim hunched his shoulders and pulled the frayed collar of his shirt up around his neck, but Papa didn't pay any mind to those busybodies, and Rose walked with her head high.

When they reached home, Papa lugged the big washtub out to the barn, and Rose filled it with hot water from the stove reservoir for Jim's bath. Papa found an old pair of his overalls, a shirt, and a pair of battered boots for Jim to wear until Mama could wash and mend his own clothing.

When Jim came shyly out of the barn all scrubbed and dressed, Rose was astonished at the change. His red hair shone, his face glowed, and his bright blue eyes seemed to be lit from within. He could have been any farmer come to town on Saturday to do his trading.

Jim stayed with them that night, and for some weeks after, sleeping in the extra bedroom. He ate heartily but politely, and kept his thoughts to himself at first, only listening to the other men talk. Papa introduced Jim to Mr. Craig and the railroad men as a distant relation who was staying until he could get on his feet.

It was a very small lie that could never hurt a soul, Papa said.

During the days, Jim helped Papa with his draywork, and out on the farm. And a little bit each day his heart began to open.

He could talk with Mr. Craig about teaching and books, but everyone wanted to hear about Cuba. No one in Mansfield had volunteered to fight the Spanish. Jim was a living, breathing history lesson, and they were eager to learn it.

Finally, one night, after everyone had pestered him, especially Rose, he told the story of the war. The other men, ignoring their cooling suppers, sat leaning forward, hanging on every word. Mama kept the door to the kitchen open, and she and Rose stood in the doorway when they weren't busy. They didn't want to miss a thing.

"The army bungled it from beginning to end," Jim said. "The newspapers made it out to be a noble fight. A splendid little war, they called it. Look how brave is the spirit of Americans.

"Let me tell you, it wasn't any such thing. It was ten thousand of us against a thousand Spaniards. And still the army made such a wreck of it, it's a miracle we beat 'em at all."

"We have been hearing about this scandal in the newspaper," said Papa. "They say the army was unprepared for such a war."

Jim said they didn't know the first thing about fighting in such a hot, humid place. The army sent the soldiers to Cuba dressed in heavy woolen uniforms.

When they reached Cuba, there was no proper way to get the horses and mules off the ships, so they made the poor beasts jump into the sea and swim to shore. Many drowned, or hurt themselves so badly on the rocks that they had to be destroyed.

The soldiers were given old rifles that took black powder, which puffed clouds of white smoke when the Americans fired them. The Spanish could easily see the smoke and knew just where to aim their own guns.

"It was just the worst sort of nightmare, impossible to describe even if I wanted to," he said softly. "No person should ever see the things I . . ." Then he fell silent. His shoulders sagged, and he stared into his plate.

No one at that table moved a muscle. No fork chimed against a plate's edge; no chair scraped against the floor; no throat was cleared. Rose's heart ached for Jim, and for all the soldiers who went to Cuba.

After a long time, he looked up.

"Why don't you eat your supper, son?" Papa said. "You've hardly had a bite. Don't distress yourself on our account."

"No, Mr. Wilder," Jim said earnestly. "It helps me to tell it. And folks need to know the truth. The truth is, the fellows that died in battle were the lucky ones. Thousands more died of jungle sickness—typhus and yellow fever—and nothing to be done for them. Not enough medicine, not enough doctors. No possibility even to ease their suffering.

"But the worst of all," he said fiercely, "was the men who died from eating tainted meat.

305

You'd think a country that calls its sons to go and die on foreign soil could at least give 'em a decent meal."

Mama turned away and dabbed her eyes with the hem of her apron. The men stared into their own plates now, silently sharing the shame.

"I'm sorry," Jim said quietly. "Now I've gone and spoiled your supper. I'm a thankless guest."

"Not at all," Mr. Craig said quickly. "We are grateful to hear the truth."

Everyone piped up that they agreed. "Yes, of course." "Don't you think twice about it, son." "Does the soul good to get it off your chest."

But Jim had talked himself out. Mama badgered him to eat and now he did, with a new hunger, as if he had broken a fever and found his appetite again. By the time Mama served the coffee, Jim's face radiated contentment. He even smiled when Mama teased him about having a fourth helping of beans.

Papa stayed true to his word. He talked to the foreman of the grading crew for the railroad, and Jim had regular work. He stayed at the house and worked on the grading crew for almost a month. He even paid Mama room and board, in spite of Mama's protests.

Then, one morning, he stuffed his few belongings in a sack and left Mansfield. He said there were good teaching jobs back east, and he meant to get on with his life. Rose went with Papa to the depot to see him off.

"Would you write to me?" Rose asked sorrowfully as they sat on a bench waiting for the train.

"I reckon I might do just that," said Jim. "Soon's I get myself into a settled situation."

"If you do, I promise I will write you back. I'll never forget you."

Jim's blue eyes looked square into Rose's, and he smiled. "You pretty near saved me from starving," he said. "I won't ever forget you either."

In late June, each day was the same as the one before. It was the time when the year seemed to be slowing down. The hot sun beat down pitilessly. When Rose walked Bunting to pasture, the cow would lumber along slowly, without stopping to nibble a bit of grass by the road. Once inside the gate, Bunting headed straight across the pasture to Fry Creek to drink and soak herself.

Fido lay panting on the bare ground in the shade of the sycamore tree behind the house, too lazy to follow Rose or chase the squirrels. Creosote oozed from the railroad ties, and the air had a tarry smell that added to the stale prickliness of the heat.

The sun scorched the grass and wilted the furry leaves of mullein until they drooped like dogs' ears. Nothing stirred. When Rose went to pump water, she had to squint against the brightness, and sweat ran down into her eyes, making them sting.

At night her attic bedroom was too stifling for sleep, so Mama let her stay downstairs in the extra room. Even so, she slept restlessly, turning the pillow every few minutes to find a cool spot, listening to the racket of chattering katydids and tree frogs.

One especially hot Sunday, as they were leaving church, Paul stepped up to Rose on the path. For an instant she thought he might ask to walk her home. Her heart fluttered, but then he said, "I rented a buggy to take Mama and George up to Wolf Creek to go swimming. Why don't you come along? The whole town's going to be there."

"I'd like that," Rose said.

"Right after dinner, then. I'll come by and pick you up."

But on the walk home, Rose began to worry. She was getting too old to wear just a thread-bare old dress that would cling to her skin when it got wet.

"You can put on one of your union suits, and wear an old dress over it," Mama suggested.

"But it's so hot. I'll just die in this heat."

"Once you get there and get wet, you won't even notice," said Mama.

Rose was miserably sweaty by the time Paul drove up in the buggy, and she felt foolish in her union suit and one of Papa's old straw hats. She didn't like for Paul to see her in such a shabby state.

But Paul and George had on their oldest holey overalls and Mrs. Cooley wore a pair of black tights under her old dress. Everyone looked rather silly, and Mrs. Cooley giggled at herself. "I could be a clown in the circus," she joked. Rose felt a bit less awkward after that.

She squeezed into the back of the buggy. The canopy threw a thankful shadow, and getting out of the sunlight, she could feel the shade as if a pressure had been lifted from her head and shoulders. She was delighted to find a block of ice on the floor next to her, chilling a watermelon. She palmed some of the cool water off the ice and rubbed it on her forehead and neck. Then Paul drove off with a lurch.

Wolf Creek was just a short way north of town. The road crossed a wooden bridge near a wide place in the creek. At the edge of a field of corn, someone had mowed the grass, and a half dozen buggies and wagons were parked there, the teams unhitched and tied under a grove of trees.

The creek was full of people, splashing and shouting. Someone had hung a rope over a deep pool, and some boys were swinging on it and dropping into the water.

George dashed off to the rope tree to play with the other boys. Rose headed straight into the water and sat down on the stony bottom, letting the water seep into her union suit and cool her all over. That was heaven, and she never wanted to move.

When Paul had unhitched the horse and tied her under the trees, he came and sat with her. Mrs. Cooley stood at the edge with just her feet and ankles in, talking with some of the other mothers who were watching their children frolic and splash each other.

"Gosh, this feels good," Paul said. "I don't think there ever was a hotter summer."

"Of course there was," said Rose. "Two years ago, when we had the drought."

"I reckon so. I forgot about that. Seems as if in the summer you can't ever think of it being cold, and in the winter you couldn't ever remember it being hot like this."

They talked pleasantly for the longest time, about everything under the sun, and agreed on most questions: whether horseless carriages would ever come to the Ozarks (no); if people would ever soar through the air in flying machines (yes); if the law would ever catch up to the famous bank robber Butch Cassidy (yes).

This was the last summer of the 1800s. In less than six months would be the start of the year 1900. Everyone had been talking about it.

"I heard some fellows uptown saying there's predictions of an earthquake at New Year's," said Paul, tossing pebbles into the water one by one. Two dragonflies, one perched atop the other, hovered above the water.

"There was a great earthquake around here a long time ago, eighteen eleven I think they said," Paul went on. "It was so strong, it changed the course of the Mississippi, and big holes opened up in the ground and swallowed whole houses."

They wondered what it must be like, to be in an earthquake. Paul thought it would be worse than even a cyclone, because there'd be no place to hide.

It was wonderful, sitting there with Paul and listening to him talk. He had become impossibly handsome, she thought. His broad, smooth forehead seemed so honest and pure. His full lips smiled easily, and he spoke earnestly in his deep voice about the future, and how he would make his way as a telegrapher. He knew the Morse code by heart now. Soon he would graduate from school and try to find his first position.

Paul was going on about it when he looked over toward the bridge, stopped talking, and frowned. Rose looked too.

A buggy had stopped there. At first Rose didn't see who was in it, but then she saw Lois in a long, sprigged lawn dress, wearing a wide flowered hat and holding a parasol. Holding the reins was a young man Rose didn't know.

Paul stared for a long moment, then sighed and looked away. The young man chirruped to the horse, and the buggy rattled away, down the road.

Rose should have kept her mouth shut, but she felt so cozy with Paul, she had to speak her mind.

"I don't see why you ever liked her. She doesn't care for anyone but her own self."

Paul stared into the water, cupping handfuls and letting them run out.

"I don't know either," he said angrily. "But I'll never forget what she did to me at the pie supper. Girls are awful scheming sometimes."

"I'm never," Rose said quickly, then blushed and looked away.

When she dared let her eyes fall on Paul's face again, he was staring at her. Rose blinked fast and she wanted to look away again, but something held her gaze steady.

"No, I guess you aren't," he finally said. "You sure are a good friend, Rose. The best of friends. You and I, we've seen a lot of things, bad and good. There isn't another soul I could talk with the way we do."

And then he looked shyly away.

Rose's heart filled to bursting with tenderness for Paul. Her chest ached with it. Her head swam, and her hands trembled. She could have blurted right out, "I just love you so much."

But instead she splashed Paul right in the face and shouted, "Best of friends, you old wet hen!"

Paul's shocked look made her laugh, and then he started splashing her back. Rose stood up to run, and Paul pushed her back down in the water.

"Who's an old wet hen now?" he cried out. Rose loved it. They chased each other around the creek for a few minutes, until Mrs. Cooley called Paul to fetch the watermelon.

Rose was sorry to end the fun so soon. But it was pleasant to sit with Mrs. Cooley and Paul and George in the grass on the bank of the creek, watching the children play, slurping the sweet watermelon, and spitting the seeds as far as they could.

That day brought back many strong and loving memories, especially of the long wagon trip from South Dakota Rose's family had made with the Cooleys. She looked at Mrs. Cooley's contented face, and at George, who could be so devilish and peevish at times, and thought how lucky she was to have good friends to share life with.

And there was Paul, who had called her his best of friends. That was a memory she would hold dear forever.

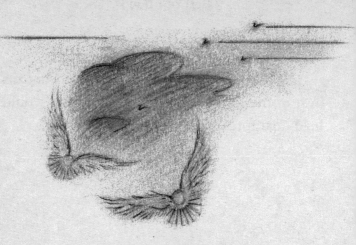

Good to Be Alive

Two mornings later Rose woke up feeling groggy and unrested, even though the weather had cooled and she had slept soundly. As she helped Mama with breakfast, her body seemed to have an extra weight to it. The dishes felt heavy in her hands.

She plodded listlessly as she led Bunting to pasture, her head feeling stuffy. She had the sensation in her chest of powdery dryness, although a rainstorm the night before had settled the dusty ground. On the way back, she coughed a couple of times, trying to get that powdery, scratchy feeling out. But it wouldn't go away.

Mama came home from an errand to find her sitting on a chair in the kitchen, resting her head on the table.

"What's the matter?" Mama said, pulling the pin out of her hat, taking it off, and setting a box of salt on the table.

"I'm so tired," Rose mumbled with a rattling cough.

Mama felt her forehead. "You are a little warm," she said worriedly. "I shouldn't wonder if you caught yourself a cold, spending all that time in your wet clothes. I told you to change as soon as you got home.

"There's a patch of mullein by the railroad tracks. Effie is always saying how mullein tea is good for a cold. I'll pick some and brew you a cup."

Rose laid her head back down on the kitchen table and closed her eyes while she waited, listening to the sounds of the door opening and closing, then Mama's fussing around the kitchen.

The tea was bitter tasting, so Mama added some sugar. It didn't do much to blunt the bitterness, but the warmth of it soothed her throat some. Then Mama put her to bed downstairs in the extra room, and Rose drifted off to sleep.

She woke to the sounds of Papa coming in, and Mr. Craig coming home from the bank. Her chest was tight, her legs tingled uncomfortably, and she began to cough. The coughing made her head throb with an ache as bad as any she'd ever had.

Mama came in straightaway and put a palm to Rose's forehead. "Poor dear, you're burning up. How does it feel?"

"Bad" was all Rose could croak out. Her throat was sore, and when she tried to swallow, she heard an echo in her head. Then a terrible fit of coughing seized and shook her hard. Every part of her hurt and ached, and she had to fight for her breath.

Deep furrows creased Mama's forehead. She left the room with a swish of her skirt, and Rose heard dimly her urgent voice. "Run and fetch

Doctor Padgett, quick. It's something serious. For God's sake, hurry, Manly."

Papa stood in the doorway as he pulled on his jacket, speaking in a hearty voice. "My prairie Rose is feeling low today, is that it? Don't you worry. We'll have you fixed up in no time." Then he shut the door and was gone.

Rose squirmed in misery. Little needles seemed to be pricking her skin all over, and knives slashed at her chest. She felt hot and clammy and threw the quilt off.

When Mama came in with a glass of cold water, she tucked Rose back in again.

"You must keep your covers on," she said. "You've got a high fever. Here, try to drink some water. It may soothe your throat a bit."

Rose slowly pulled herself up, every movement an achy effort, as if her joints had rusted and needed oiling. Mama held the cold rim of the glass against her lips. The water refreshed her parched tongue, but it was hard to swallow, and it hurt so much her hand flew to her throat. She got only a little down before another coughing fit wracked her chest.

Rose's head flopped back down on the pillow, and she closed her eyes, trying to gather back her strength. She heard the swish of Mama's skirts, the closing of the bedroom door, and her words, muffled as if spoken through cotton batting. "I'm sorry, Mr. Craig, but you will have to shift for yourself today. My daughter's quite ill, and needs tending."

He answered in a low tone that Rose couldn't make out. She wouldn't open her eyes and tried not to breathe too deeply, to keep the knives from stabbing. She also tried not to move her legs. The squirming only made the needles jab sharper.

Slowly it dawned on Rose through the haze of pain and discomfort that she was very, very sick. She had never needed a doctor before. Doctors came only when somebody was deathly ill. Now Mama had sent for one for Rose.

She could not think of herself as deathly ill. She never got more than a cold, or a stomach-ache, or a bump on the head. She had never been this sick.

She hated to cause Mama worry, all because she was too willful and strongheaded to take off her wet union suit.

Rose decided she would just get up and make the best of it. There were chores to do, and Mama needed help. But when she pushed up with her elbows and swung her legs out from under the quilt, the knives slashed, the needles jabbed, and her chest exploded in a searing fit of hacking coughs.

The door flew open, and Mama came rushing in.

"Lie down!" she exclaimed. "Where in the world do you think you're going?"

"Mama," Rose struggled to speak. "I'm sorry."

"Just you shush and be still." Mama carefully tucked Rose's covers back in. "There's nothing to be sorry for," she said gently, taking Rose's hand in hers. Mama's skin felt cool and comforting.

"You're just under the weather, is all. Anyone can get sick. You must rest and let me take care of you. Don't even think of trying to get up.

Just lie quiet, now. The doctor should be here any moment."

Rose closed her eyes again and drifted off.

Feverish dreams threaded themselves through her sleep. A piece of ice was sliding around on her chest, sending frozen bolts like shards of ice shooting all through her. She was cold to the bone, a deep, aching cold. Her spine was twisted with it, and her body was frozen solid like a Christmas ham. She fought to pull her covers tighter, but her arms were blocks of ice. She couldn't lift even a finger.

Paul splashed water on her forehead. She tried to splash him back. He laughed and laughed because Rose couldn't. His perfect white teeth flashed so bright and blinding, Rose had to look away. But she couldn't.

A voice rumbled nearby like distant thunder. Then she heard a ringing in her ears, the sound of bells, school bells. She was late for school. She would be the last one in her seat.

She hadn't studied her lessons. Mrs. Honeycutt called on her to recite. She stood, but no words could come out of her mouth. It was frozen shut. She could only moan and grunt. Blanche sat giggling and pointing at her, mocking her moans and grunts.

Cold, such a silvery cold, a snowy mist floated over everything. Mist that turned to steam. She was hot, burning up. Drenched, as if she had just gotten out of the water, or been running on the hottest summer day. She must take off her union suit. It was wet, steaming, clammy wet.

A door slammed loudly. The sound of clomping feet, horses' hooves on wood. She was in the wagon, on a ferry crossing the Missouri River. The water was boiling all around. The ferry began to sink, and Rose was drowning, sinking beneath the muddy waves, fighting for breath.

Rose slowly opened her eyes. The room was dark, except for the pale yellow light of a lamp turned low. She was drenched with sweat, and began to shiver. Her teeth chattered uncontrollably. Her breath came in painful wheezes.

She turned her head. It was so heavy, heavier than a fifty-pound sack of flour. There was

Mama, sitting in her rocking chair. Her head hung on her chest. The Bible sat open on her lap. Her hands lay at her sides, palms up, as if she were pleading.

"Mama," Rose choked out with a cough. Mama's head snapped up, and she jumped out of her chair. Her face was puffy, and her red-rimmed eyes looked fuzzy and misshapen, floating above Rose in the yellow haze of lamplight. Mama looked very big.

"Shhh!" Mama said softly. "Don't try to talk. Save your strength."

Tears welled in Rose's eyes. She wanted desperately to speak, to tell her dreams. But the knives slashed, and she shivered so violently, she had to clench her teeth. Slowly the cold released its icy grip, and she drifted off on a fleecy cloud.

More rumbling voices, and the ice on her chest. Somone had pulled the covers off and was poking her. She tried to brush the ice away, tried to brush the poking finger. Nate was teasing her, but she couldn't lift her arm to defend herself. Then Fido was standing on her chest with his little paws.

The mournful wail of a locomotive lifted her up and carried her away. She was flying high above the earth. Far below her she could see figures with upturned faces. She flew closer and saw bits of those faces. Papa's brushy mustache like a tangle of dried weeds. Mama's little upturned nose. Paul's dark eyebrows. Blanche's curly black hair. Nate's freckles. Mrs. Cooley's soft, round chin. And a pair of dark, piercing eyes all wrinkled around the edges.

Hands fluttered about her like a flock of mourning doves, cooing and rustling, their feathery wingtips gently brushing her cheeks, her hair, her shoulders. They were beautiful, those doves, and their sad calls were a kind of soft, soothing, music.

"She's better today, thank heavens," the doves whispered in Mama's voice. Rose's eyes opened slowly. The room was bright. A face was staring at her, so close she had to turn her head and squint to see it. A spray of freckles and big ears filled her vision.

"Mrs. Wilder, come quick!" Nate's voice cried out. "She just opened her eyes. Come and see!"

Mama's face floated above her on the other side of the bed. There were deep lines in her face and dark circles around her beautiful blue eyes. Mama smiled.

"Rose dear, it's Mama," she said. "How are you feeling?"

Rose smiled weakly. She wasn't hot and she wasn't shivering. Her legs prickled a little, and her chest felt sore. But she was better.

"Mama . . ." Rose's voice broke. Her throat was so scratchy, she choked on her words. "I . . . had so many . . . dreams."

"I know. You talked quite a bit in your fevers."

"Gosh, Rose," Nate said. "You were sick a long time. Days and days."

"I was?" Rose asked in wonderment. How long had she been lying there? Was it winter or summer? She couldn't tell, all bundled in her bedclothes.

"Do you think you might take some broth?" asked Mama. "I made some chicken stock, just the way you like it, with a pinch of nutmeg."

"Yes, Mama. I guess I am . . . hungry."

"Good. I'll be right back. Nate, don't you go wearing her out with chatter. See if Rose wants some water. She must be parched. But give it to her slowly."

Rose gradually got better, a little bit each day. The first time she saw Papa since she was sick, he could not speak. He just sat on the edge of the bed, holding Rose's hand, with silent tears wetting his cheeks. Rose had never seen Papa cry, ever. Seeing it brought tears to her own eyes.

"You gave us quite a scare," Papa said huskily when he could speak.

Rose wanted to spare Papa any more tears, so she said, "I dreamed about the wagon trip, when we crossed the Missouri."

"I reckon you must have had yourself quite a few dreams. You were talking a blue streak in your sleep."

There were so many things she learned in those first few days. Dr. Padgett came by, and listened to her breathing with a strange thing with tubes that he poked into his ears, and a small round metal disk that he held to her chest. Rose laughed when he placed it on her skin.

"Now that's a pretty sound," Dr. Padgett said. "If I was a sensitive fellow, I might take offense to being laughed at. What's so funny?"

"I dreamed somebody was putting ice on my chest. It was you!"

"That was me all right," said Dr. Padgett, his dark wrinkly eyes scrunched up with a smile. "No matter what I do to it, everybody complains how cold my stethoscope is."

Slowly things began to make sense again. She had had pneumonia, the worst case of it. She had been sick and delirious with fever for three whole days and nights. Everyone took turns sitting up with her, putting damp cloths on her forehead, wetting her lips and mouth to keep them from getting dry, and changing her bedclothes.

Rose was amazed at how her brain had spun crazy dreams out of real happenings.

"I dreamed I was flying once, and I could

soar up and down, and see the whole town and everyone in it," she told Blanche. Blanche rocked nervously in Mama's chair and chewed a fingernail.

"Oh, Rose. I was so worried. Everyone said . . ." She lost her voice for a moment and stared into her lap. "They said you might even die. It made me unbearably lonely to think of it. You're my best friend."

Rose just beamed. "I'm not going to die," she said. "I'm getting better every minute."

They gossiped for a long time. Blanche said Lois had been sparking with a boy from Seymour and led him on to think she would marry him, but then she started sparking with someone else, from town. The boy from Seymour got so mad and drunk, he came into town, and there was almost a shooting right on the square. Sheriff Lockwood had to arrest them both to keep from anyone getting hurt. Lois had embarrassed herself and her family before the whole town. It was a terrible scandal that Lois would never live down.

"I'll tell you a secret," said Blanche. "I don't

like Lois. Not just for what she did to Paul, but she's only for herself, and no one else."

"I know," said Rose. She felt just a little bit sorry for Lois, having her comeuppance in public. "She's so pretty. It's a shame she hasn't the manners to go with her looks."

Blanche said Paul came by twice every day to check on Rose.

"I'll tell you a secret," said Rose. "But you mustn't breathe a word to anyone. Not *anyone*."

"I won't," Blanche said, perching on the edge of the chair, her eyes dancing with pleasure.

"Well, I like Paul," Rose whispered.

Blanche squealed. "You don't really!"

"Shhh!" Rose scolded. "Of course I do. He's so sweet and thoughtful. And handsome."

"He is!" Blanche gushed. "Oh, you're so lucky to be in love, Rose. I don't think I'll ever. But does he like you back?"

Rose sighed. "I don't know. We're friends, but not like that. I'm too young yet. I'm just twelve and a half. But maybe, when I'm a little older . . ."

"I won't say a word to a soul," Blanche said. "Cross my heart."

Everyone came to visit. Paul's tenderness filled her with joy. Rose could see how worried he had been, and she was secretly glad of it. Nate came often, and one day Abe brought Effie and the babies, after Dr. Padgett said it was safe for the children. The house filled with laughter, as did every place Abe went.

Rose mended slowly. At first she could hardly lift her head without feeling dizzy. She hated using the chamber pot, but she could never get outside to the privy on her wobbly legs.

When she was used to sitting up, she sat in Mama's rocking chair and read. When she was used to that, she walked a little around her room and around the house. Bit by bit she became her old self again.

Finally the day came when Rose bathed and dressed herself in front of the chifforobe mirror. She was shocked at how thin and pale she looked. Her cheeks had narrowed, and her skin looked papery thin. But she felt wonderful, full of energy.

She went outside and turned her face to the sun and felt the gentle warmth on her skin. The air blew fresh and full of the dusty smells of late summer. She took a deep breath, and her throat and lungs didn't hurt a bit. Somewhere someone had mown hay. The sweet scent of it mixed with the perfume of Mrs. Gaskill's honeysuckle patch.

Fido nuzzled her leg. Rose crouched down to scratch his back. His right back leg jiggled the way it always did. Rose laughed. Fido smiled and gave her cheek a grateful lick.

A mockingbird landed on the clothesline and eyed her boldly, its long narrow tail twitching. The little Gaskill children were throwing a ball to each other, and next to the other side of Rose's backyard, Mrs. Hardesty was feeding her chickens.

Rose drank it all in, feeling the vibrant sounds and sights of the living world. From the depot she heard the clanging bell and labored huffing of the afternoon east-bound local leaving the station. She hurried to the back fence to watch it pass.

As the locomotive pulled into view, her heart leaped with joy to see the old engineer who had driven that same train for the last two years. He looked at Rose, and suddenly the brakes jammed on the wheels and the great smoking, steaming engine came to a halt, the cars banging behind it.

The engineer stopped the train right in front of Rose. She was amazed. The trains never stopped anywhere but depots. They had to keep their schedules.

The engineer leaned out and cried, "Howdy, young lady!"

"Hello," Rose shouted back over the panting of the boiler.

"I missed you," he said. "So I asked at the depot, and the folks said you were down mighty sick. How you doing?"

"Wonderful," Rose shouted.

"Well, you keep yourself well, you hear?"

"I will," Rose said as the engineer let the steam out into the pistons. The wheels spun for a noisy moment, then caught. The train began to move.

"It's good to be alive!" Rose cried out with all her might.

"What's that?" the engineer yelled back.

But Rose just waved and repeated it to herself. It *was* good to be alive.

Join the Little House Family!

The LAURA *Years*
By Laura Ingalls Wilder
Illustrated by Garth Williams

LITTLE HOUSE IN THE BIG WOODS

LITTLE HOUSE ON THE PRAIRIE

FARMER BOY

ON THE BANKS OF PLUM CREEK

BY THE SHORES OF SILVER LAKE

THE LONG WINTER

LITTLE TOWN ON THE PRAIRIE

THESE HAPPY GOLDEN YEARS

THE FIRST FOUR YEARS

The ROSE *Years*
By Roger Lea MacBride
Illustrated by Dan Andreasen
& David Gilleece

The CAROLINE *Years*
By Maria D. Wilkes
Illustrated by Dan Andreasen